The Puzzle Keeper

MEGAN NAFKE

ISBN: 0615567975
ISBN-13: 978-0615567976
Second Edition

DEDICATION

If there were ever angels on earth, it would by my
mother; sister-in-law, Melissa; Aunt Diane and Aunt
Lisa. I never would have gotten here without your love
and support. This book is for you.

PROLOGUE

I died five times as a child from the Watkins plague that killed a third of the world's population twenty years ago, yet I can't remember being as scared as I am right now. I stared over the 'Closed for Private Party' sign posted on the door to the Red Lion Pub, trying desperately to see if my friends were inside. After some time I peered to my side without moving and saw my boss, Gail Lewis, a large woman with short wispy brown hair and large bright brass earrings standing next to me.

"Just making sure someone was inside." I pointed at the sign on the door, as my lips stretched reluctantly into a smile.

"I'm assuming that they are inside?" Her pudgy nose flared slightly in a sigh.

"Yes, Mrs. Lewis." I opened the door and she strolled through slowly. I took a deep breath and followed her into the pub.

The small pub was filled with Survivors, which was the name given to the lucky people who had the illness during the plague but survived. Most of the people here either helped Trevor with his research on the long-term side effects of surviving the Watkins plague, or knew that he was about to make his research public. My adopted sister, Molly, loved him and his work, so I grew to tolerate him despite my knack for finding faults with anyone who dated her.

I had always known that the illness gave us some sort of side effects. Shortly after I was revived from cardiac arrest for the last time due to the plague, I started to pick up on other people's emotions, which I mimicked to my mother's frustration.

My mother thought I was simply reacting to the trauma of the illness, but then I started to see scattered images. At first the images were like trying to watch a TV show when it is flickering in and out of reception, but as the images became clear it was obvious that I was seeing other people's memories and thoughts.

Once in the bar, it didn't take long to spot Trevor, the lead researcher and Molly's fiancé. He was hard to miss since he was close to six and a half feet tall and wore oversized black retro glasses. His long, bony arms wrapped around Molly, as a crowd hovered around them. She looked up at me, her eyes hopeful, but I shook my head. I wanted to go in but I was having trouble blocking other people's thoughts and emotions; I needed to sit as far away from the crowd as possible.

My body trembled as I walked along the wooden wall filled with dart boards and ale advertisement, I could see that my body was moving down the hallway, but I didn't feel as if I was present; exhaustion was flowing through every part of my body. I fell like a lifeless rag doll into the first empty seat at the bar, and buried my head in my bare arms.

My nose twitched as I caught the strong, bitter smell of freshly brewed coffee, and saw Colin refilling a man's coffee cup a few seats down from me. From his appearance, you would not guess he was working at the pub. All the workers were required to wear a uniform consisting of a dark green shirt and black slacks, and keep their hair neatly combed. Colin, however, had on his favorite light leather jacket, tee shirt, and slightly wrinkled jeans. His chestnut brown hair was styled in a mass of unruly wave, and he always seemed two days late for a shave.

"I can't tell you how happy I am to see you," I smiled

and eagerly turned over the mug in front me.

"Are you talking to me or the coffee?" Colin asked.

"You, of course," I laughed, "though coffee would be nice."

"Uh huh," His left eyebrow rose slightly as he poured the java into my small cup.

"I didn't know you were helping out tonight," I said between sips.

"Only way Dad could close the bar for tonight." He nodded his head towards the end of the bar, where his dad was in the middle of pouring drinks.

"I can't believe Sean agreed to closing his bar," I said.

"Yeah well he'd do anything for you two," he said. Colin, Molly and I had shared a hospital room when we had the plague. Our parents became close and we grew even closer after losing four of our six parents. The two surviving parents, Colin's dad and my mom, took it upon themselves to raise all three of us. My mother even adopted Molly after her parents died, and Colin's dad tried to fill in as a father to all three of us.

"How's your day been?" Colin asked.

"Long," I took long sips of the hot coffee.

"I think we're all going to be having long days for a while."

"At least the anticipation will be over soon. Today reminds me of being at the dentist waiting to get my wisdom teeth pulled. You can't leave. You know it's going to be incredibly painful. All you can do is sit by the clock and wait for the inevitable."

"Look on the bright side. We all have each other. Some people might be going through this alone." He patted my wrist softly and looked around the room.

"True," I smiled. "I can't image how people cope with this alone."

"I can't imagine how people will feel when a tall nerd outs them on national television without any warning. I'll be back," he said strolling down to a redheaded waitress that was waving him over to the other corner of the bar. I didn't recognize the waitress and wondered if it was business or pleasure.

"Claire?" Molly asked as she slipped into a seat next to me. Molly was tall and curvy. People were drawn to her large dark eyes and winsome smile. Seeing us together most people could tell one of us was adopted.

"How's the big night going for you two?" I asked.

"It's just been the best. I've never seen him so happy." Her eyes lingered on Trevor.

"I'm glad," I said.

"You should come and watch the interview with us."

"I think I'm going to stay here and drink my coffee and watch the interview with Colin. I'll stop by later to congratulate him." Her eyes followed my gaze as I looked at Trevor. "When the crowd thins out a bit."

"Well, you do look like you need a cup." Molly put a hand on my shoulder, which felt more patronizing than sympathetic. "You look fine, sweetie." She wrapped her arms around my shoulders briefly then walked away. "I'll save you a seat at our table if you change your mind."

"You already drank your cup of coffee?" Colin peered at my cup and shook his head. "I was only gone for a minute."

"I could use another," I said.

"You're addicted to the stuff."

"I'm not addicted, I simply need to drink a certain amount of coffee a day to avoid debilitating headaches," I grinned.

"Uh huh," His deep laughter caused small ripples in the coffee pot.

Everyone stopped talking but the thoughts in the room buzzed too loud and chaotic to focus on any one thought. I turned and found everyone straining and contorting their bodies to see the screens that were placed on top of the bar.

A brunette woman in her thirties with her hair tied up in a bun was on the screen sitting across from Trevor.

"I'm here with Dr. Trevor Harris to discuss his recent

findings in his work with the Survivors," the woman said.

"Thank you, Jane." Trevor stared at something just beyond her and nodded his head. "It's been twenty years since the epidemic that killed one third of the population and left another third of the population hovering between life and death started. During the four years between epidemic cycles of the Watkins plague, most researchers have been so focused on the people that died and preventing the illness that they neglected the Survivors. In the five years since a cure has been found, most researchers have been focused on discovering how Dr. Watkins created and spread the disease. However, I have been working with the Survivors to find any long-term effects of the illness."

"And?" She asked wrinkling her brow.

"Yes, I found that certain Survivors had what I will call side effects of the illness."

"Why did only certain Survivors develop side effects?"

"I found that the majority of the people who developed any side effects were very young children at the time they contracted the illness. All the people who have side effects had cardiac arrest at least once."

"I'm not surprised that having your heart stop would cause complications, but what type of side effects did these people have?"

"That is the interesting part. As far as I can tell the side effects range in type and intensity. I've seen people who can read thoughts and emotions and people who can communicate with animals or spirits, and I've found people who can travel with their spirit." Jane looked puzzled and turned to look at something off camera.

"Those claims seem a little farfetched."

"My findings have been well documented and reviewed by the scientific community." His thin lips smiled showing his crowded front teeth. "However, I can give you a quick demonstration." He nodded his head and his research assistant came on camera. "This is Bill Mason, we're both Survivors with side effects but his is more convincing."

What do you mean?" She said but then grew very pale as the note cards in her hand started to pull away from her even though no one else was touching them. Jane jerked back and the cards hovered over her head before zooming to Bill's hands.

"Bill is telekinetic; he is able to move objects without touching them. He can give you another demonstration if you wish."

"That was enough of a demonstration for me." Jane crossed her arms and sank in her chair. "Thank you very much for coming on the show. To find out more about the research findings on the Survivors, read Dr. Harris' paper that is posted on our website."

The silence at the pub was broken when a man stood up and started clapping. I shook myself and turned my eyes away from the TV screen. The clapping was contagious and died down only as people started grabbing glasses of champagne. It's amazing how the presence of alcohol will distract people from almost anything. The tension in the room had calmed down but all I could think about was how everyone else in our town was going to take the news.

CHAPTER ONE

A tall Hispanic police officer stopped me at the gates to the mansion perched on the Santa Cruz Mountains. "I'm sorry Ma'am but I can't let you in here. This is a crime scene." He spoke as if speaking to a child.

"Yes, I know." I indicated the police tape that was only inches away from me. I handed him my badge. "I may be short and blonde but that doesn't make me a child."

"Oh, sorry. Detective Moseley told me you'd be coming." He coughed. "I just thought you'd be, older." Actually, his thoughts reflected that I would be just about anything but a petite blonde. Although he didn't mind that I was one because he was thinking about asking me out. That is until he realized from my badge that I was a Survivor. I considered reprimanding him for the political incorrectness of his thoughts but I didn't want to reveal that I could read them.

"It's all right, Officer." I signed the clipboard he was holding, and grabbed some gloves and a pair of booties.

"You made it here fast. Didn't your plane just land?" Colin asked greeting me at the gate.

"What can I say? I'm an efficient driver."

"I think police officers have another word for that: speeding."

"That's such a negative word. I prefer mine."

"I'm sure you do."

Gargoyles on the edge of the roof watched me as we walked along the stone pathway leading up to the house. Two men in casual slacks and button up shirts stood at the metallic looking front door. Their professional appearance contrasted sharply with Colin's. Colin, as usual, had on his favorite light leather jacket, tee shirt, and slightly wrinkled jeans. His chestnut brown hair was styled in a mass of unruly waves on the top of his head, and he always seemed two days late for a shave.

When we got closer to the two men, I recognized one of them as Detective Austin Hughes. My heart raced. I struggled to keep walking, as if I was wearing cement shoes.

"You could have told me he was the detective," I straightened a loose blonde curl behind my ear.

"I didn't know." Colin shrugged. "I must have talked to his partner."

I glanced up at Austin, he was still as handsome as the last time I saw him. He had broad shoulders and a short haircut like you would expect from a police officer. When I caught his gray eyes, the color of a storm cloud, searching my face, I looked away.

"Hi, Claire." Austin smiled at me. I could feel my cheeks growing hotter. "Colin." He nodded his head at Colin.

"I see you made homicide detective." I could see out of the corner of my eye that he was staring at me, but I kept my focus on the door.

"Yes, it's my third case. This is my partner, Detective David Moseley." He nodded his head towards the man next to him. He didn't look like a man who could make it as a cop, or even a round of dodge ball against a girl scout. His bones showed clearly through the skin on his face, giving him an appearance of being ill. He was no taller or wider than a typical twelve-year-old boy.

"Nice to meet you both." His voice matched his boyish size.

"It's nice to meet you, Detective Moseley," Colin said

reaching out to shake his hand.

"Better not," He said showing us his gloves. "You don't want to know what I have been touching."

"Fair enough," Colin said. "Can you give us a rundown of what you already know?"

"We figured you'd want to see the scene so we haven't moved the body," Austin said as he stepped into the house. Detective Moseley shrugged and followed him. Colin and I put on our gloves and booties and followed the detectives. Despite the house being filled with oversize windows and indoor light, it appeared dark.

Our footsteps echoed throughout the house as the two detectives led us up the long staircase. I hugged my bare arms against my chest as we walked down the chilly hallway. It felt like someone had the air conditioning on way too high. I unclenched when we stopped at a doorway.

The bedroom looked rustic like an interior of a lodge. An antique bed with maple posts took up more than half the room. A woman with long blonde hair and a white summer dress was lying across the top of the bed.

"This is Mrs. Eileen Cooper," Austin said. He indicated her open mouth. "We found what appears to be some type of material and stuffing lodged in her mouth. We haven't found the object, but we believe it's a pillow."

"What makes you think it's a pillow?" I asked.

Detective Moseley straightened. "I figured it out. There should be a pair of decorative pillows with initials embroidered on them. We found one with "BC" on it but the one with "EC" is missing."

"That's impressive," Colin said.

"Our theory at the moment is that the killer covered her mouth with a pillow to keep her quiet, and then stabbed her multiple times in the chest and abdomen." Austin indicated the stains on the top of her low cut, cotton dress.

"Wait a minute. We're in the middle of the woods. The nearest house to here is almost a mile away. Why would the killer need to keep her quiet?" Colin asked.

"That's a good question. The only explanation I could think of is that someone else was on the property or expected back," Detective Moseley said.

"What is that?" We all looked down. The word traitor was carved into the bare skin that was exposed on her chest. Each letter was deep with jagged edges.

"Traitor to whom?" Colin asked.

"We found this next to the body." Austin picked up a plastic bag with a flyer in it and held it so we could read it. It was a Brotherhood of Humanity flyer with bold lettering at the top reading, Top Twenty Most Dangerous Survivors. It was no surprise that my future brother-in-law, Trevor Harris, was number one. After all, it was his research that exposed the paranormal side effects caused by the Watkins plague. A few pictures down was a picture of Mrs. Cooper with her name written underneath. An "X" was over her picture in what looked like blood.

"Was she a Survivor?" I asked.

"No way to really tell without medical records. The husband says no, but who can tell?" Detective Moseley asked. That was true; on the outside there was nothing to distinguish us from the rest of the population and not everyone who survived the plague had paranormal side effects.

"Her son Russ is a Survivor. Poor kid's had a rough week. He was in a fight after school yesterday afternoon," Austin said.

"Where is the son?" Colin asked.

"At the hospital with his father. He had ... well I really don't know what happened to him. One minute he was crying but behaving in a normal way after losing a parent and then the next minute he completely snapped. Couldn't even understand what he was saying. We had to have an officer ride with him to the hospital to get their statements," Austin said.

"That seems understandable considering ..." I started to say.

"Trust me this was not normal," Detective Moseley said.

"We will stop by the hospital after this. Any other evidence?" I asked.

"We collected what we could. We just wouldn't know until the lab runs everything," Detective Moseley said.

"Heck, we haven't even been able to find the murder weapon. Though we think it's some type of kitchen knife," Austin said.

"Who found the body?" Colin asked after a long moment of silence.

"Mr. Cooper found the body when he came home from work, around 5:30 this evening. No one else was in the house," Detective Moseley said.

"Is there anyone else living here?" I asked.

"Her sister, Nadine, and her brother-in-law, Mike, live here as well. Mike was at work with Mr. Cooper during the time of the murder. Nadine claims she was running errands. She had a gas receipt on her with a time stamp of 4:20. She also had a receipt from Target with a time stamp of 4:50, which proves she was out of the house. We don't have the exact time of death but we do think it's around the time she was out," Austin said.

"So basically, we have a town full of suspects, with no leads and no witnesses?" I asked.

"Afraid so," Austin said.

THE PUZZLE KEEPER

CHAPTER TWO

I was on the last few sips of my cold coffee, when I heard my name being called from the nurses' station. The waiting room was filled with a sea of patients. I tried squeezing myself through a tiny gap between two tall women, but they simply pressed their hips together. Colin growled, "Move." His voice was deep and loud and made the hair on the back of my neck stand up straight. The crowd quickly moved to either side like Moses parting the Red Sea.

An elderly nurse was furiously typing on the computer in front of her. She held out her hand to the side of the computer. After a moment she sighed and looked at her empty hand, then looked up over her glasses at us. She stretched her hand closer to us and said, "Patient's card."

"I don't have one, but I think this will do." I showed her my badge and she withdrew her hand.

"What can I do for you, Agent Bennett?

A tall, curvy nurse stepped up to the counter and said, "I'll take this one. Agent Bennett is my sister." The elderly nurse looked at both of us and shook her head. I didn't have to read her mind, it was a familiar reaction to hearing we were sisters. It was obvious that one of us was adopted, since I was about as far from tall and dark as you can get. We moved out of line so we could talk privately.

"I didn't know you were back from your trip. Why didn't you call me?" Molly asked twisting the locket around her neck.

"I just got home, haven't even picked up Rosie yet. Besides, I figured you were busy moving in with that fiancé of yours."

"You know I'm never too busy for you, sweetie."

"It seems we are both busy these days. You move out to be with Trevor, and I spend my time cleaning up his messes." The image of Mrs. Cooper's body popped into my head.

Molly ignored me and turned to Colin and pointed her finger at him, "speaking of work. She just gets back and you put my sister to work. Can't you do a case without her?"

Colin stopped playing with his cell phone and looked up, "When has she ever listened to me? The words 'No' and 'can't' are like catnip to her."

"I know, I'm just teasing." She gave him a quick hug. "I don't get to see you much anymore so I need to get in as much teasing as I can. I know this isn't a social call, what are you guys doing here?"

"I think the more important question is what are you doing in the E.R.?"

"No, choice." She shrugged. "The whole hospital has turned into one big emergency room."

"Is it safe for you to work here? What if someone dies near you?" I asked.

"I've been careful. My boss is working here tonight, too. She's aware of my problem. She has assigned me to work triage."

"Still seems rather risky," I said. Molly normally works in a clinic, where the chance of being around when someone died was slim. The closer she is to a person when they die the better the chance a ghost will know she can see them and the more they stick around and bother her.

"We are here checking on a patient. Was Russ Cooper seen here?" Colin asked.

Molly scanned the computer screen and then said, "Yes, he was moved to a room for the night."

"How is he?" I asked.

"We talked about this. You know I can't tell you," Molly said.

"I'm sorry. I know. Can we speak to him?" I asked.

"Depends. It's up to his doctor and his father if he is up to talking. Let me give them a call," she said. After a short phone conversation, she said that Russ' father agreed to speak to us and gave us the directions to his room.

We made our way to Russ' hospital room on the eighth floor. A large bald man who resembled a short-tempered nightclub bouncer stood outside room 305.

"Mr. Cooper?" He nodded and I shook his hand "I'm Agent Claire Bennett and this is my partner, Agent Colin O'Connor," I said as Colin shook his hand.

"I don't understand. Why are you here? The cops have already been here to talk to us." His voice reminded me of a drill sergeant.

"We work for the Bureau of Survivor Affairs. You probably haven't heard of it. It's a relatively new agency that deals with cases that involve the Survivors. We have been assigned to your wife's case because some of the evidence points to it being a Survivor related crime," Colin said.

When Mr. Cooper didn't say anything I added, "We are very sorry for your loss. How is your son?"

"It took two hours to calm him down," he said. "It was so bad they're making him stay the night, just in case it happens again."

"Losing a parent can be very painful," I said.

"No, it was different. It wasn't just sadness from losing his mom although that is bad enough. I haven't seen pain like that since the army. Let me tell you, nothing in the world is worse than seeing your child in pain and not being able to do a damn thing to make it better." Mr. Cooper took a seat on a tiny chair propped against the wall and buried his head in his hands. "I think he blames himself for the murder."

"Why do you think that?" Colin asked.

"My son has always been," he paused and scratched the small bald spot in the back of his head and finally said, "Different. I always liked that about him. Since the news came out, he has been more different than usual."

"Is different bad?" Colin asked.

"Now it is. Haven't you seen the papers?" Mr. Cooper asked. We nodded. The image of the bombing of a Survivor support center in upstate New York popped into my head. It didn't take much to provoke violence. Being different right now was dangerous if not deadly. "He is a walking target, from the costumes he wears to telling everyone he meets that he has 'magical powers'."

"I could see how that'd be a serious problem," Colin commented.

"You don't know the half of it," Mr. Cooper said. "Can you imagine being at the grocery store and having your son tell the teller, a complete stranger mind you, that he is able to steal memories?"

"That would be a bit awkward." I swallowed a laugh. I liked the boy already.

"Is he really able to steal memories? Or is he just a telepath or something?" Colin asked.

"Just a telepath?" His face stiffened. "Oh God, I hope not."

"Excuse me?" I asked. "What's wrong with being a telepath?"

"There's a difference between someone that does not like telepaths and someone not wanting their loved one to be one," Colin said.

Mr. Cooper nodded in agreement, but by his thoughts he wasn't entirely sure why I was angry. Colin put a hand on my shoulder. I looked up at him and relaxed. He was right. For the most part I liked being a telepath, but I wouldn't like someone else using it on me.

"Just tell us what you do know about Russ's abilities," Colin said.

"Russ says he sees things when he touches objects.

Things that aren't really there. To be frank, He doesn't talk about this stuff to me and I don't ask. Maybe I should have."

"How has he handled being so open about his side effect?" Colin asked.

"He found out the hard way why it was a bad idea. A group of kids jumped him on his way home from school. It was so bad I had to take him to the hospital for stitches." I noticed his neck muscles twitching just above the collar of his white polo shirt. "Ever since then he has locked himself in his room glued to the computer."

"Did you try talking to him?" I asked.

"I tried. I really did. My wife was the one he talks to. I mean talked to," his hazel eyes became red and glossy. "Eileen would've known what to do."

"You're not alone." I put my hand on his thick shoulder. "We will find a way to help him."

A croaking voice called "Dad?" from inside Russ' room.

"We can talk about this later. Come see us when Russ gets released." Colin handed him his business card.

Thankfully, my apartment wasn't far from the hospital. I could hardly wait to see my dog Rosie, take a shower and get the stink of the airport and crime scene off of me. From first glance the boutiques and restaurants that line my street, Cherry Blossom Lane, look like stylish cottages from some small European village, each painted a different pastel color. The upper stories of each building had apartments. Light glowed ahead, leading me to the one store still open. My eyes blinked as they adjusted to the light as I gazed into the Wonderland Bakery. It was aptly named. The walls had murals of scenes from *Alice in Wonderland*, and the tables and the chairs were funky enough for the Mad Hatter's tea party.

I could see Alice's frizzy black hair bounce as she danced from the oven to the counter with a batch of cupcakes. Alice froze when she saw me. Redness spread across her creamed coffee skin. She gestured at a plate of frosted sugar cookies shaped like bunnies. My stomach growled at me to take the offer.

It had become a test of wills to live over the bakery, the smell of chocolate flowing through the apartment.

"Glad to see you back, girl," Alice said opening the door to her shop and embracing me with a hug. "Rosie's been missing you. I never knew a dog could pout that much."

"Thanks for watching her. Would have asked Molly but you know …."

"I was glad to do it. How was the trip?"

"It was another case of a neighborhood overreacting to the discovery of a Survivor with side effects in their midst. By the time I got there the murderer had pretty much identified himself by bragging to anyone who'd listen how he got rid of 'that freak down the street'. Not much need for a telepath there."

"Now don't go making me sorry I made that appointment with that reporter."

"What reporter?"

"While you were gone, the local news team decided to do a series of stories about the Survivors and they asked for volunteers. So, I volunteered."

"Why would you do that?!" I shook my head in exasperation. "Have you not been listening to the kind of problems Colin and I have had to deal with since the news came out about our existence?"

"If all people hear is what's wrong with us how will anything ever change?"

"Well, yes, but your timing couldn't be worse. I'm on another Survivor related murder and this time it's local. And it looks like we've got an active anti-Survivor organization calling themselves 'The Brotherhood of Humanity'. Can't you postpone it?"

"You worry too much. I'm a baker; who would hurt a baker?"

"When is the interview? I want to be there to scan the crowd for problems."

"It's Friday night. I appreciate you coming down for it.

Speaking of my special goods, I have some dream cookies all ready for you to take home." She disappeared into the kitchen.

Alice's side effect centered around baking. She made many types of cookies with various effects, but my favorite was the dream cookie. It allowed you to take complete control of your dreams. You could relive memories so vividly it was hard to separate the true memory from the dream or allowed you to make any dream scenario feel real. Although you had to be careful to eat them before bed, or you risk dreaming while awake. For that reason, she only sold or gave her special baked goods to a select few.

Alice reappeared and handed me a pink box. "I'd better get back," Alice said over the oven buzzer.

"Thanks again," I said.

Alice nodded and gave me a quick wave as I walked alongside the building to the door of my apartment.

Rosie, a border collie with German shepherd coloring was pouting in the living room when I opened the door. It would have made me feel guilty but her bushy tail was wagging behind her. When she decided I'd suffered enough, she got up and walked over so I could pet her. I noticed a light was on in Molly's room. For a moment I had a jolt of happiness and went to look for her. When I got to her room, it was empty except for the furniture and I remembered that she moved out while I was gone. It was the first night Molly has lived away from me since we shared a hospital room as kids. Rosie and I curled up on her mattress and we fell asleep.

THE PUZZLE KEEPER

CHAPTER THREE

Steel and glass covered the ten-story office building that loomed high above the one-story shops that lined the streets around it. Unfamiliar men in uniform greeted me at the garage gates. Sam, a former Army sergeant with silver hair and sharp narrow nose greeted me when I entered.

"Good morning, Sam," I said hugging him.

"Hey, be friendly on your own time, Claire. Some of us like to get to work on time," Tom said from behind me. Tom had the muscular body of a football player. He was well groomed, from his trimmed nails to his gelled-up hair. He could have been a model, if it wasn't for a large scar that ran from just below his left eye to his chin.

"Ma'am," Sam's normally cheerful face stiffened. His face softened into a smile when we walked a few feet away from Tom.

"All this security seems a bit much for our first week in the new building."

"Didn't you hear about the fire?" Sam asked, processing my small briefcase through security.

"Which one? I heard about several on the radio this morning."

"Is your job too complicated? Just give her the bag and then put my briefcase through the machine," Tom said, craning his thick neck.

"Tom, wait your turn," Sam said. "I figured you already

21

knew about Trevor's lab seeing as you're friends with him."
He coughed. "Our old field office was set on fire."

"Was anyone hurt?" I asked.

"No, Ma'am. Had everyone cleared out of the office before the news came on."

"So does that mean we were leaked to the media?" I asked. The only people who knew about our old office and what we did, were the people who worked there and a few government officials. Our families didn't even know about our work.

"No. Someone leaked the location of Trevor's lab. They didn't make the connection to anything else going on there. Thank God they didn't know we all moved to another building when the news hit."

"How did you know that Trevor was the target?" I asked.

"Almost all the damage was isolated to his lab," Sam said.

"Poor Trevor, he is really having a hard time since he went public with his research," I said. Before I could say anything else a loud alarm went off.

"Tom, I told you to wait your turn," Sam said walking up to Tom.

"You should have just let me through, old man," He said staring down at Sam who was a good foot shorter than Tom. "It's not like you're a real guard. All you've got to do is check my bag and let me through."

"I think this calls for a body search," Sam turned his head and winked at me. "You can go on ahead. I think Tom will be here for a while."

Gail, my boss, was tapping her watch with her short stubby finger from the doorway to her office when I walked into the Primary Case Division. I rolled my eyes, when I noticed that the time reflected I was one minute late. I clutched my briefcase as I weaved in and out of the small wooden desks that cluttered the room. I dropped off my bagged lunch in the kitchen nook that we all shared, before making my way to my office.

My office, which I shared with Colin, was one of the few window offices that surrounded the room. Colin was already at his desk sorting through stacks of office supplies.

"You're here early," I said noticing that he had already unpacked two boxes of old files. I repositioned the small golden plaque with my name on it that sat on my empty desk. It was going to take a while to get used to having a real office. Up until now, we spent most of our time traveling from case to case. So much so that home felt like a vacation.

"I thought it'd be good to come in early for our first day in the new office. Coffee?" I peered up and saw Colin holding a large traveling coffee cup that read, "Don't talk to me until my coffee is down to this level", with a line at the halfway point of the cup.

"How did you know?" I took the coffee cup and smiled.

"From years of being around you in the morning before you had coffee."

"Glad to see you were able to find your way to work this morning, Agent Bennett," Gail said as she swung our office door open. Before I could comment, she added, "Mr. Cooper is here with his son."

"Where?" Colin asked scanning the office room behind Gail.

"Down on the second floor, in the psychiatry office."

"I didn't know we had a psychiatry department," I said

"Why is he there?" Colin asked.

Gail raised an eyebrow as if to say, "you idiot". "We had to add one. There are too many people that have been diagnosed as insane, but are really just experiencing side effects. We start everyone off there so we can properly diagnose them."

"I can see the need for that," Colin said and I nodded. We have had a handful of cases of people locked in mental institutions, because they believed they were hallucinating instead of really seeing things other people couldn't.

"It also runs as a normal psychiatry department. If you

ever need someone to talk to." Her eyes lingered over me and I fidgeted in my chair. Sometimes I think that it would be a good idea to talk to a therapist. The constant stream of raw emotions I experience from people I meet in this job can be draining at times. Unfortunately, in my case it would be a waste of time. For one thing I have recently completed a masters degree in psychology and I couldn't imagine what they could teach me about how to cope with my ability that I didn't already know. Not to mention the fact that knowing what your therapist is thinking about while you sharing personal information, is not something I want to experience.

"All right, we will take care of it," I said.

"What a good idea." Gail glared at us both and left the room without saying goodbye.

We decided that I would talk to Russ alone, and Colin would talk to Mr. Cooper in our office. It was easier to focus my telepathy if it's just one person in the room.

I entered the waiting room of the psychiatric department and found the room crowded with patients, the majority of whom were reading out of date magazines with extreme focus. Even with it being crowded in the waiting room, the patients had at least three chairs between each other and a few chose to stand at various spots rather than sit in the available chairs. It felt as if I was in an ER waiting room where everyone in the room was afraid of being next to someone who was contagious with a deadly disease.

"Russ Cooper," I yelled loudly.

"Yeah," a deep exasperated voice said from the back of the room.

A tall bony teenager stood up in the back row of the waiting room. His outfit made him looked like he was an actor from a low budget version of one of The *Lord of the Rings* movies.

"Russ, it's a pleasure to meet you," I said.

"Let's get this over with." He scowled at me.

When we reached the interview room, he used a large

wooden walking stick to slowly make his way to the sofa; his long even strides made me think that he used the walking stick as a prop for his outfit rather than an aid in walking.

"Before we start, I want to warn you that I'm not a therapist. My job is to solve your mother's murder. Anything you say in here is not confidential, if it relates to the case or your safety. That being said I think I can help you."

"I don't see why I had to come," Russ said as he took a seat on the sofa and started to straighten the floor length cloak over his lap.

"After talking with your dad, we felt it might be beneficial for you to come talk to me. Why do you think you're here?" I asked.

"I don't know." Russ said as he rubbed a finger along the edges of the cloak. "I guess it's because I'm different." I'm guessing different was an understatement, but it didn't seem harmful to him or anyone else to dress up in costume.

"I hear that you've dressed up in costume ever since the news has come out about the Survivors." I looked at his ears and pointed to them. "Are those elf ears?"

"Yeah, I mimicked how my character looks in *World of Warcraft*." He smiled and twirled his stick on the floor. "I'm a high-level mage in that game."

"Why did you want to dress like your character?" I asked.

"I don't know ...." He looked at me intently. "I'm not crazy."

It was typical for a Survivor to state that they were not crazy. Crazy is such a strong and destructive word. While I see Survivors dealing with an array of emotional crisis, I don't believe any of them are truly crazy. It would be hard to think of anyone as normal or average, so I prefer to think that people are different degrees of unusual.

"Your father says that you have been telling people that you have magic powers." He shuffled his feet and stared at the small rock waterfall that sat on the round table in front of him. When he didn't respond I added, "He also told me that you see things that others can't."

"I don't care what anyone says. The things I see are real." His deep voice was slow and steady, but I could feel raw rage start to build in him and my own body mimicked the rage as it flowed in me and made my heart rate quicken. I was finding it hard to block his emotions, as scattered images flashed in my mind of him being laughed at and hit by a group of teenage boys.

"What type of things do you see?" I asked.

"Why, should I tell you? You're just another person that'll tell me I'm not crazy but write that I am in my file." Russ lowered his voice. "The only ones that do believe me are the guys online."

"You should tell me because I'm like you. I see and hear other people's thoughts. I see their memories and feel their emotions. I know what it's like to not have control over it. I can help you if you let me." I looked him straight in the eyes and gave him a steady nod. I could feel the intensity of his anger fade and my heartbeat went back to normal.

"What magic ability do you have?" I asked.

"I looked it up online it's called psychometry. I'm able to touch objects and see memories or sometimes just emotions from the people who used the object." He paused deep in thought. "At first it was scary, I could not stop the images from appearing and I saw events that I didn't want to see." I still struggle with keeping other people's thoughts out of my head, it's like being in a nightmare you desperately want to escape but you can't until you see the whole scene.

"Was your mother's death one of the events you didn't want to see?"

"Yes." Russ closed his eyes and shook his head as if he was trying to shake the memory away. "I can still hear her scream."

"I'm sorry, Russ." I put a hand on his cold bony wrist.

"It's ok."

"It's not ok. I know how hard it is to not be able to

control it, to not be able to make the thoughts and images stop." After a few moments Russ nodded. "Let's start with you telling me what happened yesterday after you got home."

"My dad picked me up on his way home from work. When we got home I sat down to watch some TV before dinner. A few minutes later my dad screamed and came running downstairs. He told me to stay where I was and called 911. He said mom was dead and after that it's pretty much a blur. People came in and out for a long time. While I was sitting on the curb, I noticed something blue in the gutter and picked it up. That's when I saw my mom's body. It was horrible and I couldn't make it stop. The next thing I remember is the hospital." Russ shivered.

"I'm sorry I have to ask you this but we need to know in more detail what you saw and if possible, whose eyes you were looking through. What did you pick up?"

"It was a ribbon. I dropped it as soon as I saw my mother's body so I only got a flash of that image which I wish I'd never seen. I can't stop hearing her scream." Russ was paler than normal, which was like going from pale to paler. "Will I ever be able to stop hearing it?" He looked into my eyes, and I saw past the surly teenager and saw a scared boy.

"I'm going to be honest with you. It's going to take time. You're going to have to stay away from objects that give off memories of your mother's death." He sunk deep into the sofa. "One day it will not hurt you as much as it does now."

"I sure hope so."

"It was very brave of you to come here today and share your vision with me. I know it must be very painful for you. I will do everything I can to find out what happened to your mother."

"I had to. It's my mom," he said as he straightened his robe and left the room.

The moment my foot stepped into my office, Mr.

Cooper asked, "So does he really see things?"

"Yes. Though you'll be happy to know he isn't a telepath," I grimaced as I said it. "His ability is psychometry, that is, he can read other people's memories from objects they have handled. It's what set him off yesterday. He saw memories from the murder."

"What did he see?" Mr. Cooper asked.

"While I'm not bound by confidentiality rules, I think this is something Russ should tell you himself," I said.

"I had hoped to spare him from seeing his mother like that. What can I do for him? How can I protect him?" Mr. Cooper asked.

"I have arranged for you and Russ to stay in our temporary sanctuary on the fifth floor. Russ can get help with dealing with his mother's death, and with controlling his ability," I said.

"More to the point, he might be in as much danger as his mother was. This is simply the safest place he could be," Colin added and Mr. Cooper nodded.

"You've got to be kidding me." Russ grunted as we stepped out of the elevator. The fifth floor, labeled as "Survivor Haven", was drastically different from the other floors. The halls were covered in neon pink and green, and each of its big rooms was painted a different color and theme. In the middle of the fifth floor was a huge room filled with people roaming around or sitting at what looked like art tables spread around the room. This room served as the dormitory at night and the living space during the day.

"It's not so bad," Mr. Cooper said. I was impressed that he was able to say it with a straight face.

"Yeah, if I was a five-year-old girl this would be just perfect." Russ hunched his shoulders and dragged his feet as we made our way across the large room.

A group of girls who couldn't be more then ten years old were painting paper butterflies at one of the tables. They all wore matching pink shirts that said, 'princess'. As I walked past them I noticed one girl slightly taller than the rest twisting her hair with her left hand and waving at me with her right hand. I waved back. When she came closer, I groaned when I realized it was Abby.

"Nice outfit," Colin said.

"It helps them open up to me," Abby shrugged.

"It sounds like a fun job," I said. I cringed in regret when I realized what I had said.

"We need some extra help down here with the children if you're offering. I'll even get you a matching outfit." Her tiny pink mouth curled in a smile. It was hard to say no to her. Abby had the ability to identify other people's feelings and to manipulate them. I knew she was trying it now. I felt happier.

I was about to say yes when Colin woke me out of my euphoric haze, saying, "That's not a good selling point for me."

"Aww but you'd look so cute in pink," Abby said.

"Why are you guys down here?" Abby asked moving us all to the wall away from the children.

"This is Mr. Cooper and his son, Russ. They are going to be staying here," Colin said. "I think Gail called you earlier?"

Abby squinted her eyes and after a moment they became large with comprehension. "Oh, yes. I'm so sorry. We've had so many new people today that it's hard to keep track of everyone. Though I think you'd stand out." Abby touched Russ's robe.

"It's ok," Mr. Cooper said. "We're just happy to be here. Right Russ?"

"Ecstatic," Russ said in a monotone voice.

"Just go down there." Abby pointed to a desk with a tall young man propped up in front of a computer screen. "He will get you organized." As they were leaving she added, "Welcome to our humble abode."

Colin explained their situation when they walked out of earshot.

"Oh the poor thing." She shook her head. "I will keep

an eye out for him." With Abby's ability to manipulate emotions, she could help bring Russ back if he gets stuck in a painful memory of his mother's death.

"Call me if he is having trouble or remembers something," I said.

"I will." She touched my arm softly and then rejoined the group of girls at the art table.

"Well, well, well. If it isn't Dorothy and her little dog, too," Tom said when we entered the kitchen nook.

"You'd better watch it," Colin said approaching Tom's table.

"Or what? You're going to chew my shoes?" Tom asked.

"Do I need to remind you two that we are at work?" I pulled open the fridge, and searched though the stacks of plastic containers.

"I never would have guessed you two worked here. I just finished my third case." Tom yawned. "I wonder how many have you two solved."

"It's not a competition," I said.

"No, you're right. You'd have to solve a case first for that."

"I just came back from a case I solved," I said.

"That's not how I heard it. I understand the guy confessed before you got there," Tom said.

"We have solved plenty over the last couple of years," Colin said his voice getting louder and deeper.

"But as you know they don't count. Even if it did, I still solved more than both of you." Tom was right. Only Gail knew about the cases we did before the news, and she didn't want the public to know what we have already done, because it would show that the government knew about us years before Trevor's announcement.

"It would have been tough for us to solve as many cases as you did, considering we were still in school and you were already on the force." Colin and Tom continued to snap at each other. I was only half listening as I ransacked the shelves and counters in the kitchen nook.

"Ah hah!" I said picking up my empty container that was soaking in the sink.

"The lunch gremlin is back?" Colin asked looking at Tom, who was smiling. Most people look nice when they smile, but on Tom it looked unnatural and almost creepy.

"I was hoping it would stop. I was looking forward to it all morning," I said.

"Pity. It's almost as sad as having an over-glorified security guard confiscate my gourmet lunch," Tom said cleaning his nails with a napkin.

"You ate my food? It had my name on it, Tom," I said.

"Not saying I did. But maybe this is a lesson. You take something from me, I will take the same from you."

"I didn't do that to you," I said.

"Don't do it again, Tom." Colin stepped right in front of Tom's face. "I only give one warning."

Tom smirked and threw his soda can in the garbage. "Don't make promises you can't keep, Lassie." He left the room with a smile on his face.

"One day he is going to go too far." Colin reached in and grabbed a paper wrapped sub from the fridge.

"It could be worse. He could pull rank and make us work as his assistants." I shuddered.

"Don't even think that," Colin said. "We just need to solve something big or they will keep on treating us like we're just some college kids."

"It'd be nice to wipe that smug look off his face," I said.

"I'm sorry, about your lunch." Colin broke off half his sub and placed it on a napkin in the spot beside him. "You've got to start bringing in bad food for lunch. No one will go after that."

"Thanks."

"No problem."

"Learn anything interesting from the father?" I asked biting into the soggy roast beef and cheese sub.

"Not too much. Found out that before the news she

didn't have any enemies. Mrs. Cooper was a stay at home mom. She financed and ran fundraisers for a long list of causes. Most of which had to do with plague research and support groups." He took a big bite of his sandwich. "The interesting part was that Mrs. Cooper was the prime backer for Trevor's research in the early stages," Colin said between bites of his sandwich.

"That helps explains why she was on a list of Survivors, when there's no proof she is one." I had no idea that Trevor had financial backers besides the government. I wondered how many people were involved in his research.

"You've got to feel bad for the guy," Colin said.

"What I'm more worried about is if we don't figure it out soon, Russ could be the next one on the killer's list. His mom might be a supporter of Survivors, but Russ is one."

CHAPTER FOUR

When I got home from work, I unlocked the doorknob, but found the deadbolt unlocked. The hairs on my arm stood on end. I shook myself. I must have forgotten to lock it. I swung the door open, but after seeing the lights in the living room on, I took a step back.

"Hello? Is anyone there?" I tilted my head into the door to listen, but the only sound in the room was a radio humming. Rosie poked her head into the entryway and whined. I grabbed a large umbrella, which stood against the frame of the front door. When I passed the kitchen my nose caught the familiar, sweet smell of freshly baked chocolate chip cookies. I relaxed and put the umbrella down on the floor.

I followed Rosie down the narrow soft blue hallway to Molly's room. I knocked on the door. When no one answered I asked, "What did Trevor do this time?" No one answered, but I could hear a raspy, off-key voice over the radio.

I opened the door, and saw a man well over six feet tall singing into a wooden hair brush and dancing on Molly's bed like he was struck by lightning. When he turned around and I saw his trademark black retro glasses, I recognized Trevor and the fuzzy pink robe he was wearing was mine. He tumbled off the bed, when he saw me standing at the doorway to the room.

"What do you think you're doing?" I asked. Trevor stood up and clutched my robe over his blinding white legs that were covered in patches of bushy black hair. "Are you naked?"

"I … uh … didn't you talk to Molly?" He turned off the music and put down the hairbrush he had been using as a microphone.

"I'm going to go with no." I glared at him, and he shrugged his shoulders and smiled. I threw my arms up and stormed out of the room. I searched the house for Molly. It was a fast search since we only had two bathrooms, three bedrooms, and a big open space for the living room and dining room that was separated from the kitchen by a wall with a large pass through. When I got to the living room, I didn't find my sister, I found a tall police officer, stroking Rosie's stomach. I sighed, "Some guard dog you turned out to be." The police officer heard me and looked up. Every inch of his body was hard and filled with muscles; even his face had a strong cleft chin. I would have felt intimidated, but his light brown eyes and long eyelashes seemed soft almost childlike.

"I'm Officer Myers, ma'am," he said.

"What are you doing in my apartment?" I turned from Officer Myers to Trevor who was standing in the hallway. "Well?"

The room was so quiet that we all heard the rustling of keys. Molly put the laundry basket down as she walked into the kitchen. She peered out of the large kitchen pass through into the living room.

"Oh, I'm glad I caught you," Molly said.

"Before what? Before I walked in on your fiancé wearing my clothes or before I ran into a strange man in my living room?"

"Oh, poor Trevor." She peered through the pass through at both men.

"Poor Trevor?" I sputtered. "What about poor me? You promised me that he wouldn't come here until things settle down."

"I know. I'm sorry," Trevor said from the archway into the hallway. He was pulling the robe close to his body and looking down at his feet. He was making it hard to stay angry.

"Why don't you both go and watch some TV?" Molly asked. Trevor shuffled off into the living room and perched on the edge of the sky blue sofa. The police officer tried to sit in the matching recliner, but Rosie was already curled in it. I heard him thinking of making her move, but he didn't want to find out the hard way if she was a friendly dog or not. Instead he sat as far away as he could from Trevor on the same couch.

"I'm sorry. I know he is your fiancé. But we had a deal," I said.

"He didn't have anywhere else to go." Molly's voice lowered and she said, "His landlord kicked him out after finding out about what happened to his lab."

"That just proves my point of why I don't want him here until things settle down." She wilted at my words so I put my hand on her shoulder. "Don't get me wrong. I like Trevor, and I'm sorry this happened to him. He should be somewhere he can be better protected."

"What would you want me to do?"

"I don't know, but there has to be somewhere else he could go."

"We will all be safe here. He has police protection." Molly indicated the police officer sitting on the couch.

"How did he swing that?"

"His research with the government has made him both an asset and a liability."

"How long?" I asked.

"They said they could move him to a safer place in a few days. They're just finding it hard to find a safe place for him."

"You mean other people aren't eagerly wanting to have him stay at their place?" I let my mouth drop. I had a feeling it was going to be more than a few days. I liked Trevor, and even I didn't want him staying here.

"Play nice." Molly made her scolding face. However, it was hard to take her seriously when she wore her Muppets themed nurses uniform and had her dark brown hair pulled back in a ponytail.

"I make no promises." I glanced over at Trevor who was pulling on my pink robe trying to cover as much as he could. It was a full-length robe on me but barely came to his knees. Meanwhile the police officer was inspecting his own hand pore by pore trying not to look in Trevor's direction. I stifled a laugh. "Why can't he stay at the Haven?"

"We tried, but there are a lot of Survivors already taking sanctuary there. Apparently, he has little love from either side. We weren't there ten minutes before a group of teenagers started a fight with him." She took out the tray of cookies from the oven. "It's not just them. Almost every Survivor we've seen in the last few weeks blames him for their misfortunes."

"I'm sorry." I couldn't think of anything else to say.

"Do you want one?" Molly held out a plate of chocolate chip cookies.

I reached out for a cookie but quickly withdrew my hand. "Only for a few nights?"

"Only a few nights."

"I can live with that." I picked up a cookie and I could feel its warmth and the gooey chocolate chips melting in my hand.

"Why is he wearing my clothes?" I asked after eating a few bites of my warm, chewy cookie.

"I didn't leave any clothes here that would work even if I am taller than you. Your long robe was the only thing that came close to covering him. He's only going to wear it until his clothes are washed."

"No, he can keep it." I shivered with the thought of wearing that robe against my skin. "What happened to his clothes?" I asked.

"You don't want to know. I'm going shopping to get us new clothes tomorrow. I'll add a new robe for you to my list."

Molly had to work a late shift at the hospital but she was able to meet me at the Red Lion Pub on her break. The pub was conveniently located a few blocks down the street from my apartment toward the hospital. Colin's dad, Sean, owned the pub and since he welcomed Survivors it was quickly becoming a Survivor hangout.

As I turned the corner to the pub, I noticed two men in matching white dress shirts and dark pants handing out bright yellow flyers behind a small table with a sign that read, "Brotherhood of Humanity". I tried to walk past them, but the taller of the two stepped in my way. He was at least six feet tall, which is a good nine inches taller than me, so I stopped.

"For your safety, I'd advise you not to go in there, miss." His breath reeked of garlic and vinegar as he bent down to whisper, "They're supporters of the Survivors."

"Really?" My mouth dropped and I let out a gasp. "How do you know that?" I asked stepping away from his face to get some fresh air.

"They had a party in honor of the freak, the night he revealed what the disease turned them into." He sounded as if he was speaking of common knowledge.

"Thank you for your concern." I put my hand on his arm trying hard to sound sincere. "I wish I knew about this before, but I'm afraid I'm going to have to go in. I have someone waiting for me inside."

"Take this." The shorter man next to him handed me a flyer. The flyer read: *Know the truth about the Survivors before it's too late.*

I laughed the minute the door swung shut after me.

Molly wasn't in our normal seat by the fireplace but I spotted Sean stacking mugs behind the bar.

"I was wonderin' when I'd see your pretty face, lass." Sean still had a trace of an accent even though he'd left

Ireland before Colin was born.

"Seems a bit tense in here."

"No more than usual for a Monday," He said after assessing the room.

"Even with the protesters outside?"

"Well, they seem to be attractin' more business than scarin' it off. But as long as you're here, I wouldn't mind if you'd keep a listen out for any trouble that might be brewin'," he said with a wink.

"I'll do that."

"Colin got you a table in the back where it's a bit more private. You'd best get along now so we don't have to listen to Colin whine about not being fed regular."

"No, we wouldn't want that."

As I passed the wall separating the front of the pub from the rear dining area I could see Molly and Colin sitting at our table. My stomach fell when I turned toward the table and saw Trevor.

"What's he doing here?" I asked.

"I thought he could use a night out. I didn't think you'd mind," Molly said.

"I do mind. Did you not see the men outside? What if they see him and follow him back home?" I asked.

"We came in the back way," said the man in the booth next to them. When he put the menu down I noticed it was Officer Meyers. "They can't see us from the window."

"There's still a chance he will be seen," Colin added. He nodded his head towards the end of the bar, where Sean was pouring drinks, more into his own glass than into the glasses of the customers he was serving. By the way his mustache was wiggling and his arms were gesturing, he was clearly in the middle of one of his stories. "I'd be very unhappy if anything happens to Pop's pub because you came here."

"I'm with you. I'd rather stay at home, but until it becomes a safety issue for him being in public, he calls the shots," Office Meyer said.

"If it becomes an issue, you leave by the back way and if

you can't get back into my apartment without being seen, you can just drive to the Haven," I said sitting down reluctantly next to Trevor. Trevor didn't say anything only nodded.

I wasn't used to being tense in the pub. It was one of my favorite places. I loved the way Sean had made it look like a pub from the old country. It felt like home filled with stories and laughter, until Trevor ruined it.

Our waitress arrived to take our order now that we were all there. She was the new redhead that served us the night of Trevor's announcement.

"Hi Brittany, this will be an easy order," Colin said. "We'd like one of every appetizer, a pitcher of beer for the guys, an ice-tea for Molly and coffee for Claire." Colin pointed to the table next to us where Officer Meyers sat. Officer Meyers had his back to the wall and was too busy scanning the room to see Colin's gesture. "He's a friend of Trevor's. Bring him whatever he wants. On the house."

"Can you make the coffee decaf?" I asked, after realizing that it was too late to have my usual drink.

"You're just so sweet," Brittany said, replying to Colin and ignoring me completely. In fact she hadn't looked at anyone except Colin, since the moment she reached the table.

"Just don't tell anyone." Colin's grinned and winked at her. She raised her note pad to cover her cheeks that grew redder by the second.

"Oh, I would never do such a thing." She giggled. This was quickly becoming a poorly written teen romance movie. I made a gagging gesture towards Molly and she laughed.

"Anything else I can get you, Colin?" she asked with a smile just for him. Colin shook his head.

"Thanks, Brittany," Colin said.

"Did you write down the decaf?" I asked politely but more firmly than before. Brittany's back stiffened and she clutched her hands tightly over the pad of paper. She didn't respond or turn around, but simply walked to the bar swaying her small bony hips.

"What did I ever do to her?" I asked.

"Who? Brittany?" Colin asked turning his attention away from watching the waitress. I nodded. "I don't know what you're talking about. She has always been nice to everyone."

Molly and I rolled our eyes at each other. "If by everyone you mean just you. Then yes she is a very nice girl," I said.

"It sounds like someone's a little jealous," Colin said.

"Jealous? Of what?" I just want to have a waitress that listens to my order. Is that too much to ask?

"Maybe we should just talk about something else," Molly said. I glanced at Molly who had put her long arm across the table to hold my wrist.

"Hey sorry to hear about your lab," Colin said.

"I meant a less sensitive topic." Molly put her hand over her eyes and sighed.

"What'd I say? I'm just saying I feel bad for him."

"Nothing. I appreciate it," Trevor said.

"Did you lose anything important?" Colin asked.

"We lost most of the data on the new genetics research we had just started," he said.

"What about genetics?" Colin asked.

"Well, not everyone who had the plague has side effects. I'd like to determine if genetics plays a part in developing side effects. Is there a common gene among Survivors with side effects? For that matter, did genetics play a role in who lived and who died? Then there is the emerging field of epigenetics. Are the new special abilities dormant in most people and if so, how did their switches get turned on?"

"I remember my mom saying that when she studying shamans and shamanism, that most shamans seemed to have some trauma in their early life prior to their first mystical experience, but not everyone in the tribe that had a traumatic experience in childhood became a shaman.

Is this related?" I asked.

"I'm aware that there are some theories floating around that link childhood trauma to alleged psychic abilities, but nothing that has been rigorously studied. Part of the problem has been the rarity of individuals who would qualify for such a study. With the plague there is no shortage of subjects and there is a wide range of new abilities."

"If this has to do with genetics, will the abilities be passed to the next generation?" Colin asked.

"If it's caused by either a permanent mutation in a gene or a gene switched on via epigenetics, it very likely it will be passed on. However, we are just getting started with the research so nobody knows yet." It was just getting interesting when Brittany came back with our drinks.

"Decaf?" I asked.

"Sure," Brittany flipped her hair and smiled at Colin. I cringed as I took a sip. Even a person who didn't drink coffee would have known from it's potent taste and smell that it was not only caffeinated but had a few extra scoops thrown in to make it stronger.

"Colin, those guys outside are trying to stare through the windows," Brittany said.

"I'll take care of it if they come inside. Otherwise, looking doesn't hurt anyone," Colin said.

I took a quick scan of the patrons' minds but they were all pretty quiet. Most were Survivors wishing Trevor had never made his research into Survivor side effects public. A few were angry about the exposure and were thinking of what they might do to Trevor if they ever got a hold of him. In the best scenarios it was a quick death.

"It's so nice of you to protect us," Brittany said.

After Brittany left, Colin stood up from the booth and went forward to get a look at the fellows handing out flyers. When he came back, he reassured us that the booth couldn't be seen from the window.

Brittany brought us a big tray full of every appetizer on the menu from extra spicy Buffalo wings to fried mozzarella stick oozing with melted cheese. My mouth watered as she put the plates in the middle of the table. As she left, Colin sat up a little straighter and started sniffing the air. At first I thought it was the food, but then he said, "Get him out of here."

"What?" Molly asked.

"Now. Through the back." Colin didn't have to say anything else; Trevor practically pushed me over to get out of the booth, his oversized retro glasses sliding down his nose. Officer Myers put a hand on Trevor shoulder and led him to the kitchen.

Colin shook the table as he leapt out of his seat. "I'll be back."

I turned around and saw the two protestors walking towards the back of the pub. Colin walked toward the two men while his dad came out from behind the bar.

The taller man said, "We know he's here, where is he?"

"Who?" Colin asked.

"You know who," he said.

"Leave," Colin said in such harsh tone that I felt a shiver go down my spine.

"It's a free country," the taller of the two men said crossing his arms and smiling.

"That's right, it's a free country. I'm free to decline service to whomever I want," Sean said.

"You better watch your mouth, traitor." The tall man tapped a finger on Sean's chest.

"Traitor?" Colin asked. "You might want to look up that word in the dictionary before throwing it around."

"I know what it means," he glared at his companion who was laughing. "You're harboring that traitor to humanity and that makes you one of them."

"What makes you think I'm not one of 'them'?" Colin asked.

"Boy, you just made a big mistake," he said.

"I will say it one more time before I throw you out," Colin walked up so close to the man he could have kissed him, "leave."

At this point, every other man in the bar rose to his feet and started to move behind Colin and Sean.

"You made an enemy out of the wrong man." The protestors walked to the doorway and stopped, "They can't always protect you. If the traitor doesn't leave soon, you will regret it. I promise." He smiled and left the pub.

"A round o' drinks on the house," Sean said and a cheer went up from the crowd.

Colin helped pour drinks before coming back to the table.

"I think I'm going to go," Molly said, her body shaking like a leaf stuck in a fan. "He's not going to let Trevor come back in here."

"You both can stay as long as you want. My dad won't let anyone tell him who he can have in the pub and who he can't."

"That's not it. I need to check on Trevor before I go back to work," she said.

"Do you want me come with you?" I asked.

"No, you stay," Molly said.

"I'll see you at home," I said as Molly bent down and hugged me before leaving through the back.

I was relieved to feel the cool breeze nip my face as I left the pub. I stayed long enough to hear the Celtic band's first set. Now the music that had been blaring inside the pub was just a hum of vibration. The only real sound out here was a cat scurrying along the alleyway. My body flinched as a hand grabbed the bare skin on top of my left shoulder. I swung around, fist clenched, but before I could swing my arm forward, a hand clutched my fist.

"It's just me," Colin said. "I actually wasn't trying to scare you, this time."

"Uh huh. A likely story." I rolled my eyes.

"No, honest. I tried to get you on the way out." He showed me the sheer green scarf he was holding. "You left this in there."

"Oh. Thank you." Colin wrapped it around my neck, letting a part of his hand graze my neck. I could feel the hairs on my neck tingle, and a rush of warmth surged through my body. I shook myself, and we both took a step away from each other.

"You aren't walking home are you?" He nodded his head down the dimly lit street.

"Do we really need to go through this every time?" I asked. Colin crossed his arms and stared down at me. "I live six blocks away. It seems silly to drive."

"Let me walk you."

"I'll be fine. I'm not scared to walk alone. It's not like anyone other than you could sneak up on me." I pointed to my head and he nodded.

"Pop wouldn't be happy if he finds out, and his lectures like his stories never change."

"I'm willing to take that chance. It might be the last chance for quiet for who knows how long."

"I get it, just don't tell Pop." He hugged me against his chest. I relaxed against his warm body. I could smell the leather of his jacket and a faint hint of lime from the drinks he poured. "Call me if something happens with Trevor or you need to get away from him."

"Thanks," I said pulling away from him.

My heels clinked on the pavement, in rhythm with the rushing water of the marble fountain of cherubs and the flickering streetlights creating an urban melody.

I saw something dart just out of view next to me, my body stiffened and I turned thinking it was Colin trying to scare me. After a quick scan of the streets and alley, I only saw a gray cat pouncing on something down the side street next to me.

I wrapped my hands tightly around my chest. I felt like running, but I forced myself to walk at a normal pace.

A police officer I didn't recognize was sitting on my sofa watching T.V. when I got home. He filled his uniform like an overstuffed scarecrow whose buttons were on the verge of breaking with every move.

"You must be Ms. Bennett?" He asked walking into the entryway.

"Yes, I am." I bent down to stroke Rosie's neck as she sat on the tops of my feet. "And you are?"

"I'm Officer Olsson. I'm one of the officers protecting Dr. Harris." He bent down to pet the top of Rosie's head but she growled at him. The officer wiggled his blonde mustache and stepped back. "Is she friendly?"

"She is." I was surprised. Colin had the ability to communicate with dogs, and he had trained Rosie specifically to only be aggressive if she senses danger. I tried hard not to read people's thoughts off the job. But in this case I was willing to make an exception.

"God you give one speeding ticket to your boss's wife and this is what you get. If Bella didn't need braces I'd quit this job. Nothing's worth putting my neck on the line for these freaks. Should've just let them die like they were supposed to back when they got sick." he thought.

"It's nice to meet you." Officer Olsson, held his hand out to me.

"Likewise." I took his hand and felt his seething disgust for me flow into my body. I looked up into his black and sunken eyes, and a chill ran down my back.

"Night," I said in a squeaky voice.

"See you in the morning. I will be out here if you need anything." I shuddered and walked down the hall keeping an eye on the living room. When I made it to my bedroom, I locked the door and put the desk chair under the doorknob. It was going to be a long night.

THE PUZZLE KEEPER

CHAPTER FIVE

Two days later, Rosie and I were still hiding out in my room when Mr. Cooper called. He was at the funeral and was having problems getting Russ to go inside. I told him I'd be right there and called Colin to let him know where I was going. Luckily my black suit was clean and appropriate for attending a funeral. When I got to the church, I spotted Mr. Cooper pacing on the front porch. I stepped in front of him when I reached the top of the stairs. He stopped abruptly and blinked a few times before noticing me. "I'm sure glad to see you, Agent Bennett. Abby couldn't leave the Haven and I don't know how to help Russ."

"What's the problem?"

Mr. Cooper nodded his head toward a bench on the lawn where Russ was sitting with his back to us.

"He doesn't want to come in and he won't tell me what's wrong. He can't miss his mother's funeral."

"Let me see what I can do." I could hardly recognize Russ out of his Middle Earth gear. If he wasn't so sad, he'd be quite handsome in his suit.

"What are you doing here?" He asked.

"I just came to check on you. Your dad is worried about you and the funeral can't start without you."

"I don't want to go"

"Is it too hard to face the reality of your mom being gone?"

"No, you just don't understand. I still keep seeing her body and I don't want to get any more images stuck in my head."

"If you can't handle it, I'd be happy to take you back to the Haven."

"I can't do that to my mom. She deserves to have me there. And I don't want to let my dad down either."

"I understand how difficult this is for you. I had a hard time going to my dad's funeral when he died from the plague. Would you like me to come with you?"

"I guess that'd be ok. Can you stop me from seeing anything else?"

"The only way that would happen is if you don't touch any objects that are connected to your mom's murder. It doesn't seem likely that there are any objects here that you need to avoid except the coffin."

Russ thought it over for a minute and then shrugged and nodded his head. "Dad asked for a closed casket and I'm not one of the pall bearers, so I guess I can try."

We walked back to the porch and I told Mr. Cooper that I would be sitting with Russ and that he was to avoid touching the coffin. He looked relieved and gave Russ a hug. As we approached the family pew, I saw that there were two people already sitting there, a woman with leathery, tanned skin and bleached blonde hair and a short, burly man in a suit. He was good looking and looked exceptionally fit but I was not getting a good feeling about him. He started to preen when I looked at him.

Mr. Cooper said, "I'd like you to meet Nadine Foster and her husband Mike, Russ's aunt and uncle."

"I'm very sorry for your loss," I said.

"Thank you." Nadine smiled revealing her yellowing teeth.

"Was she your sister?" I asked.

"My baby sister. The only sibling I had left after the plague." She shook her head and looked down.

"It's all right, babe," Mike said patting her leg. "You still got me." That would have made me more depressed, but it seemed to make her swoon with delight.

The service was short but well attended. Mrs. Cooper was well loved and active in her community. As long as I was there, I thought I would scan the thoughts in the room. If the murderer was here he might betray himself by his thoughts. Most people were thinking about how much they would miss Mrs. Cooper or had concerns for Russ and his dad while a few were wishing they were somewhere else and hoping it would be over soon. Those people who wished they were elsewhere had seen too many funerals as we lost a third of the population to the plague over the last 20 years. They would never get used to funerals no matter how many they attended.

Mr. Cooper and I waited with Russ for everyone but the pall bearers to file out of the room. The chatter died down as people left the room except for the elderly pastor, pall bearers, and the family. With fewer people in the room, I realized that I could hear something that wasn't a thought. It was like a cell phone breaking up. I tried to focus on each person in the room but I couldn't tell where it was coming from.

I walked with Russ behind the pallbearers as they carried the coffin down the small paved pathway to the graveyard. The pallbearers didn't get more than a few feet before having to stop and set down the coffin. The oldest pallbearer, a man in his sixties, braced himself on a tree and held his hand over his left chest.

"I'll get some help," Mr. Cooper said.

"Just give me a minute," the man said wheezing between each word. "I'm apparently as old as my children tell me I am."

"I don't think it's you this ..." Russ's uncle started to say.

"Take all the time you need," Mr. Cooper interrupted indicating Russ with his eyes. Russ's uncle hmphed. I was glad he stopped him before saying anything because based on his thoughts he was about to make a crack about Mrs. Coopers weight, which was odd since she was rather slender.

"Ok, I'm ready to go on," said the wheezing pallbearer.

We had not gotten more than another 10 feet before the oldest pallbearer stumbled and let go of the coffin. Without his help to hold it up, the others were forced to let it go also. Like a scene from a horror movie, the coffin lid opened and two bodies rolled out. I grabbed Russ's arm and turned him around. I was hoping he wouldn't have an additional scene that he just couldn't forget. I peered around Russ's body to see what was happening. I could see that the other body was that of a dark-haired woman. Mr. Cooper and one of the pallbearers had righted the coffin and were putting Mrs. Cooper back in. I thought I heard the same broken voice that I'd heard in the chapel but I couldn't find it. The thoughts of the crowd buzzed too loud and chaotic for me to focus on any one thought.

I turned to take Russ back inside when I heard someone say "Dear God, this woman is alive!"

I handed Russ off to his dad and went to work. As I pushed my way through the crowd around the body I could hear people calling 911. When I got to the front, Pastor Doyle, the elderly pastor, was covering her with his coat. I was shocked by the woman's condition. She almost didn't look human because she had been cut up so much. I identified myself and asked everyone to step back but not to leave until the police had gotten their information.

"I'm going to stay with her," Pastor Doyle announced. From the look in his eye, I could see that it was futile to try to move him. I crouched by the woman and took her hand. Her skin was very cold. It took me a moment to find her pulse it was weak and thready. There wasn't anything I could do for her other than hold her hand and wait for the paramedics. While I was waiting, I called Colin with my free hand and asked him to get the detectives here as soon as possible.

"Do any of you recognize this woman?" The crowd

went silent.

Then Mike Foster replied, "I wouldn't recognize my own mother if she was cut up that bad."

The paramedics arrived a few minutes later and had an easier time getting through the crowd than I did. While they were taking vital signs, I spotted, Colin, who was now a white and grey wolf gliding down a row of headstones towards me. As he came closer, his body became misty like fog drifting towards me. No one else seemed to notice Colin, which was not a surprise, since I have not met many people who could see either of the spirit realms, living or dead.

"Glad to see you here."

"Thank you," said a voice behind me. I turned my head and saw Austin and Detective Mosley. As the paramedics placed her on the gurney, Detective Mosley asked, "What are her chances?"

"She is alive but barely; we've got to go now. You can meet us at the hospital"

"I'm coming with you." Pastor Doyle scrambled into the ambulance and sat next to the woman. Both the paramedics blinked at each other. "Well are you coming or not?"

The paramedics grumbled but one climbed into the back with the pastor. "There's no more room for anyone else. We're headed for San Jose General, if you want to follow us."

Detective Mosley caught Austin's bewildered expression and said, "Officer Hanson can go now and I'll go after we've secured the scene, meet me there when you're done here." He headed for the church with a couple of uniformed officers.

"Where's Colin?" Austin asked.

I glanced down at Colin who was sitting next to me. "He's running late."

"I see, well it will be nice to spend some time working alone with you. Not that Colin is bad to work with. I mean

…." I caught Colin rolling his eyes.

"I know what you mean. It's nice to work with you, too." After explaining what had happened at the funeral, we decided to question the youth pastor, Pastor Johnson, who had assisted the reverend with the service. We wanted him to guide us through movements of the coffin before the service, while the forensics team worked on the crime scene and the other officers took the guests' statements.

He walked us to the hearse that was parked in the small parking lot at the back of the church. He guided us along the path the coffin took from the hearse through a small stone pathway to the back doors into the parlor.

"The body was not moved after that?" Austin asked.

"Not until after the service," Pastor Johnson said. Colin tracked the trail with his nose and when he reached the spot where the coffin had sat in the parlor he turned around and nodded.

"Did anyone check the coffin when it made it here?" I asked.

"Yes, I did. She was the only one in there when she came in."

"How could Jane Doe get into the coffin?" Austin asked.

"No, clue I was in the building the whole time," he said. Colin was sniffing around the corner so I followed him. When he reached the side door he pointed to it with his nose.

"Through that door?" I asked and Colin nodded.

"I don't know since I didn't see it." Pastor Johnson replied somewhat puzzled.

"Oh, sorry I was just thinking out loud." The one down side of being able to see Colin is that it results in making me look like I was crazy. I could tell that the pastor was having doubts about me from the look he was giving me.

We interviewed the rest of the funeral mortuary and church staff in a makeshift interview room in the chapel next to the sanctuary. It didn't hurt to interview our witnesses in a place that encouraged them to tell the truth. The interviews didn't turn up anything unexpected. As far as the staff was concerned, it was a perfectly ordinary funeral. The only person to have access to the coffin other than the staff was Mr. Cooper who had asked for a few minutes alone with his wife about an hour before the funeral started. While we were interviewing the staff, Colin continued searching the church in spirit wolf form to see if he could smell anyone who didn't belong. He poked his head in the room and shook it when he was done. By that I assumed he meant that he hadn't found anything.

We held the immediate family for the last of the interviews hoping we would have something positive to tell them. They were waiting for us at the choir room.

As we entered the room Nadine leapt up, interrupting Austin as he was about to greet them.

"We've been here for hours."

"I know. I'm sorry about the wait. We'll make this as fast as possible," I said.

"Good," Nadine said.

"We need to know your movements prior to the start of the funeral," Austin said. "Let's start with you, Mr. Foster."

Austin and Mike moved to the first row so that Austin could take his statement. I was going to follow him but I caught a glimpse of Colin coming into the room. I waited to see if he needed anything but he started smelling each person in the room. I scanned the room and saw that Russ was tracking Colin's movements with his eyes, which were now like saucers. I moved next to him and whispered, "That's Colin. We'll talk about him later at the Haven." Russ nodded without taking his eyes off of Colin. He relaxed a little so I moved away.

"Does anyone know who the girl in the coffin is?" Austin asked.

"Blondie over there already asked us that," Mike said pointing to me.

"We wanted to ask again after everything calmed down.

There's a good chance that Mrs. Cooper either knew the girl or the murders are somehow connected," I said.

"That ridiculous, the two aren't connected," Nadine said.

"How do you know that?" Austin asked.

"I …" she coughed. "I need to get my cough drops. Will you be a dear and get my purse, Russ?" She pointed to a sparkly bag on a chair across the room.

Russ didn't say anything but stalked off.

"Thank you Russy," she called after him. Russ paused momentarily and took a deep breath.

Russ screamed dropping the purse and turning towards Nadine.

"Russ?" Mr. Cooper asked bolting for him.

"You knew!" Russ ran lunging at his Aunt Nadine. Austin caught him with one arm around the waist. "You were there when my mom was killed."

"Russy, I wasn't home. I wouldn't hurt my sister."

"Liar!" Russ growled. Russ lunged at Nadine again. "Claire, tell her she is lying. She saw him."

"Is Russ right? Did you see someone?" I put my hand over her left hand.

"No," She said. I cleared my mind and an image of a man kneeling over Mrs. Cooper, carving into her chest flashed in my mind. Just before the man turned around so I could see his face she ripped her hand away from mine.

"Let's just hear what she has to say," Austin said.

"I trusted you!" He screamed at me, his voice cracking.

"Russ, …" I started to say but Russ started screaming again clutching his ears. "It won't stop."

"I'm stopping this." Mr. Cooper grabbed a hold of Russ's arm and pulled him back. "He's been through enough."

"We'll talk to him later at the Haven." My heart sunk as Russ glanced at me before leaving, I could see the redness in his eye as he held back tears.

Colin met Austin and me in front of the hospital. We

found Detective Moseley and Pastor Doyle in the waiting room of the ICU. The detective told us that Jane Doe was in surgery to relieve a subdural hematoma. We all didn't need to stay and wait for hours until she got out of surgery, so I volunteered to stay with Detective Mosley and the pastor, who refused to leave. By the time Dr. Ramos came out the three of us were the only ones left in what had been a crowded waiting room. The news was mixed. Jane Doe pulled through the surgery but was still in a coma. He said that they would be better able to assess her condition in the morning.

I stayed and let Detective Moseley go since he had a family who needed him. I took the chair by her bed, and the minster took the cot the nurses brought. I held her hand hoping it gave her some comfort.

"Claire?" I opened my eyes, and my heart skipped a beat, when I couldn't remember where I was. I saw Jane Doe and relaxed. I turned around and saw Molly in her nurses scrubs.

"You can't be here," I said.

"I won't stay long." She placed a blanket over my shoulders and a small lunch box on my lap. "I just needed to check on you. I heard from a couple of nurses on this floor that you haven't left not even to eat."

"I just couldn't leave."

She put a hand on my shoulder. "I understand. But you can't forget to take care of yourself. If you need anything just ask."

"Wait," I said when she started to head towards the door. "Could you try talking to her?"

"She's not dead," she said raising an eyebrow.

"She's somewhere in between. I can't read her enough to make out any words."

"What do I do? The spirits I see aren't connected to bodies."

"Try touching her. It helps me read thoughts and it couldn't hurt."

Pastor Doyle woke up with Molly moving past him to stand next to the hospital bed. He didn't say anything but watched Molly as she bent down and held Jane Doe's hand. Molly jerked her head up as if she saw something just behind me. "Her spirit is flickering, but she's here."

"Can you hear her?" I asked turning around but not seeing what Molly was looking at.

"No but she's giving me images. Something about a flower, and ummm ... she's protecting it."

"A flower? What about the person who killed her?"

"I can't see, it's so blurry. Wait, she's showing me a man with a scary mask on. I can feel fear."

"Tell her I won't let anyone hurt her," Pastor Doyle said. "I won't leave her."

"I think she heard you. Oh, I lost it; she's fading too much, which in this case is a good thing. It means she is less on the edge. I'm sorry that wasn't very helpful."

"They're all pieces to the puzzle. That's how my telepathy feels, I have all the puzzle pieces but I just can't see the whole picture."

As long as we were both awake, I shared the food Molly had brought with Pastor Doyle and then let him go back to sleep.

I must have fallen asleep because the next thing I knew, Dr. Ramos was removing the ventilator.

"Dr. Ramos, how is she doing?"

"Surprisingly well. She is still in a coma but she is able to breathe on her own. We are hopeful that she will wake up. We don't know when. It could be today or not for another month. Perhaps you two should think about going home."

"I'm not leaving. I promised her," declared Pastor Doyle.

"Well, I do need to see Russ today. I'm really glad you are staying with her, Reverend." I was relieved that Jane Doe was out of immediate danger. I was so afraid that it would be my fault if she died. I should have recognized that there was a living person in the coffin. I knew the sound was important and I should have spent more time trying to figure out what it was.

Colin picked me up at home after I showered and changed clothes. We found Mr. Cooper and Russ in the Survivor Haven. Mr. Cooper stood up from the chair he was sitting in when he saw us walking towards them. He gestured with his hand for us to stop and came towards us.

"How is he doing?" I asked.

"He is upset and angry. He's not talking and I'm really worried about him."

"Can we talk to him?" Colin asked.

"You can try, but don't take it personally if he doesn't respond."

"We won't." I smiled.

Russ was stretched out on a cot basking in the afternoon sun that was pouring through the window above him. His was the only cot still set up in the room. The rest had been put away for the day.

"Do you mind if we sit?" I asked. Russ pretended he didn't hear me and picked up a *Spiderman* comic book and held it in front of his face.

"We need to talk about what happened yesterday," I said.

"You mean when you betrayed me?" He was radiating so much anger and hurt it was hard for me to concentrate.

"We can't accuse your aunt of hiding who hurt your mom without evidence," Colin said.

"Did you get any?"

"Not evidence, but we did get a lead from your aunt's response to your accusations."

"What did you find?" he asked, sitting up.

"I can't tell you right now, you'll have to trust me that we're making progress. You were a big help in getting this lead. By being there, you made her think of what happened."

"I guess that's something. I just don't get them," he muttered.

"I can understand that. I frequently don't understand why people do the things they do," I said.

"But they're not just somebody. They're my family. Didn't you see how they looked at me?" He slammed his comic down on the cot and then looked shocked. Russ picked it back up and examined it carefully looking for damage.

"I know it's tough to lose your mom. I lost mine, too. On the bright side, we both have fathers that love us. There are a lot of kids in this room who don't have anyone." Colin swept his hand over the room that was filled with children and teenagers and very few adults.

"Yeah. I guess. Still hurts. Can't think of anything else. I keep having flashes of my mom. Her screams. I just can't sleep."

"Do you have something of hers that would give you a happy memory if you held it?" I asked.

Russ searched his bag under his cot and pulled out a small box. "She gave me this last month, for my birthday." He opened the box that contained a black watch with a silver face.

"It's beautiful." I smiled putting my hand on his wrist. "Next time you have a painful memory, hold the watch. If your ability is anything like mine, it will force you to experience the memory of the watch."

"It's worth a try." He slipped the box in his robe pocket. "Thanks, by the way. For an adult you're ok."

"You're welcome." That was probably the highest praise a teenager could give.

"We also need to talk about the other thing you saw yesterday."

"Dude, that was so cool! Are you really a ghost wolf?"

"Spirit wolf. I'm not dead yet," Colin said with a chuckle. "I can see ghosts when I'm in spirit wolf form but not normally."

"Am I going to see ghosts now?"

"Not if you're like me. I can see the spirits of living people in the spirit realm but not the dead," I said.

"You mean there are more than just you?" Russ asked.

"Yes, there are quite a few Survivors who walk in the spirit realm. Not all of them are wolves. We don't know why people are different forms. I didn't "choose" to be a wolf, I just am one."

"Yes, but with you, I think it may have something to do with your ability to communicate with dogs."

"You can talk to dogs?!" From his thoughts, talking to dogs was even cooler than being a spirit wolf.

"Russ, have you ever thought about having a dog?" I asked.

"I've always wanted one but my mom was allergic to them."

"If your dad doesn't object, I think you should have a dog. My Rosie helps me cope on days when I'm overwhelmed by other people's thoughts or emotions. I can't hear her thoughts and she gives me simple, uncomplicated love. I think a dog would help you to cope after you have touched something with unpleasant memories attached to it."

"I'd be happy to help you pick out a dog that is just right for you. I picked Rosie for Clare and trained her special to take care of Clare and her special needs. Your dog should be able to knock an object out of your hands if it is causing problems and to keep you safe from bullies who don't understand your gift."

"Plus you'd be able to touch your dog and have nothing but happy memories," I said.

"I've never gotten memories from touching an animal," Russ said.

"Your dog's collar then," I said.

Seeing that Russ was animated drew Mr. Cooper over.

"Dad, can I have a dog?"

"Russ, we don't even have our own place to live anymore. I'd be more than happy to let you have a dog once we find a new place."

Colin took that as a "yes" and went to interview puppies for Russ after he dropped me back home.

Austin called to tell us he was on his way to the hospital, because Dr. Ramos called saying they had a suspicious person trying to see Jane Doe.

"Thanks, for coming so fast," Dr. Ramos said as he met us at the hospital security desk. He walked to the closed door behind the desk. "She's in here."

"Who is she?" Austin asked.

"No clue," the doctor said. "She refuses to talk to anyone but the police. She didn't even have ID on her. I thought you might want to talk to anyone lurking outside Jane Doe's hospital room."

"You did the right thing …" Detective Mosley stopped talking when the doctor opened the door. "That's your lurker?" he sneered. I stifled a laugh when I caught sight of her; she looked like a stereotypical preschool teacher, not much of a danger to anyone.

Austin nudged Detective Moseley into the room, "Thanks for calling us. We can take it from here."

The security guard that was sitting across from her folded up the magazine he was reading and walked to the door, "Have fun."

"Why were you outside Jane Does hospital room?" Austin asked.

She shook her head. "Credentials first." We all got our badges and put them on the table.

"Survivors huh?" Her small button noise twitched.

"Is that a problem?" Colin asked.

"We'll see." She pushed our credentials back towards us. I closed my eyes trying to catch her thoughts, but found she was singing, "It's a Small, Small World" repeatedly in her mind. How did she know?

"And who are you?" Austin asked.

"For today you can call me Mary Smith," she said.

"Where's your ID?" Detective Mosley demanded.

"I left it at home. Last time I checked, it's not a crime to not have an ID."

"All right, Miss Smith, Why were you outside Jane Doe's hospital room?" Austin asked.

"I saw her on the news. Her face was too scared for me to know for sure, but I think I know her. I just need a good look at her."

"Why didn't you just tell them that?" Colin asked.

"Because I couldn't risk it. The people I help need to stay hidden."

"Who do you protect?" Detective Mosley asked.

"That isn't why I'm here. Do you want me to try and identify Jane Doe or not?"

"Let's start by going upstairs and seeing if you can identify the woman, and then we can try to sort this mess out," Austin said.

A large curtain surrounded the hospital bed of Jane Doe. There was a silhouette of a man slumped in the chair next to the bed. Beneath the curtain we could see that the TV remote had slipped out of his hand and was dangling close to the floor. He woke up with a sharp snore when we came closer and stood up alert. "Who's there?"

We were about to answer but Pastor Doyle was already peering out of the curtains.

"What is she doing here?" Pastor Doyle asked. "I had her removed," he said pointing to Mary Smith.

"It's all right." I put a hand on his shoulder. "She wasn't here to hurt her. Only to see if she knows her."

He opened the curtain so we could enter.

Mary Smith stood over Jane Doe and hesitantly touched the scars running down her cheek.

"Do you know her?" I asked.

"In a way." Her voice softened. "I run a shelter for women and children escaping dangerous situations since the news."

"So taking in women who are running away from their husbands because they are survivors?" Colin asked.

"When it's necessary," she replied.

"I bet," Detective Mosley snorted.

"You don't call this necessary?" She asked him pointing to the woman in the bed. No one had anything to say. "She came to us a little over a week ago. I don't know much about her other than she called herself Susanna Russo, but I doubt that's even her real name. She really opened up to her roommate, but I'm not sure even she knows Susanna's real name."

"Her fingerprints aren't in the system and we have no way of finding out who she is. Can we talk to her roommate?" Austin asked.

"We don't let men in our shelters, and she's too scared to leave. I guess I could arrange to take Agent Bennett to the shelter with me tomorrow."

"You do know she's a Survivor?" Colin asked.

"Yes, which is why she'll have to be blindfolded."

"Let's just take her downtown and find out who she really is," Detective Mosley said.

"If you do that, your possible witness will disappear. The shelter will disband and everyone will be sent on to other safe houses," she said.

"Besides, we have no grounds for taking her in. She is obviously cooperating as much as she can without endangering the shelter," Austin said.

"Why don't we have coffee in the cafeteria and make arrangements for tomorrow?" I asked.

When I got home, Molly and Officer Myers sat in the dining room drinking coffee and gossiping about the hospital. In only a matter of a few days, Officer Myers had already fit nicely into our dysfunctional family. He did the dishes, gossiped with Molly before she went to work and rubbed Rosie's belly while we watched TV.

"So what's the news today?" I asked.

"Shouldn't we be asking you that?" Trevor sat on the

sofa, wearing Batman PJ bottoms and a black shirt with coffee stains down the front.

"Don't start," Molly said.

"What are you talking about?" I asked.

"Ignore him. He's a bit sensitive about the news," Molly said.

"Sensitive? Mrs. Cooper was about to be buried with another person in her coffin and I have to find out about it from the news when you were there!"

"You're low on the list of people I need to worry about. I have a teenager who lost his mother and a young woman fighting for her life in the hospital."

"You could have left me a note."

"When the body count from your mess drops I'll do that." I regretted it the moment I said it. Trevor stormed off to his room and slammed the door.

"Great! I just got him to start eating again." Molly got up and walked down the hall. "It doesn't take a telepath to see how devastated he is over the consequences of his research. I don't know how you could have missed it."

CHAPTER SIX

The next day I waited in Alum Rock Park for Mary to pick me up. She had not given me a specific time so that she could check the park and make sure no one was with me before revealing herself. She arrived on foot and we had a fairly long walk to her car. When we got to the car, she opened the backseat door and before I could slide in Colin, in spirit wolf form, leapt in.

"I should have seen this coming," I said quietly to Colin.

"What?" Mary asked, looking around.

"Nothing I just saw a stray mutt."

She handed me a long piece of fabric. "Is this really necessary?" She crossed her arms and watched me put on the blindfold.

She didn't talk to me the whole trip; instead she played music from that radio that drowned out the sounds of the street. The only clues I had to where we were going was the smell of pine trees that are typically in the mountains.

When she turned off the engine she said, "You can take it off." We were at a large country home with a small barn and pasture. I opened the door and Colin jumped out with me.

"How many people have you got here?" I asked.

"Enough." This was going to be a fun conversation.

"I'm having you meet her out back. Some of the women would be scared off by you." She led me around the house.

"Yes, I do look like the dangerous type." I laughed.

"It's not funny. I've got a woman running away from a sweet looking girl like yourself, who made her hallucinate being tortured and killed."

"That's awful." I hadn't expected anyone using their ability in such a horrible way.

"There's victims on both sides." She led me to a small white gazebo that overlooked a small playground. A woman who wore a long-sleeved blue shirt and jeans sat on the porch swing inside the gazebo. It was too warm a day for long sleeves and I wondered what she was hiding.

"Agent Bennett, this is Laura. Do you need me to stay?" Mary asked.

"No, you go on ahead inside." The woman smiled and pointed to the empty seat next to her.

"Thank you for speaking with me," I said sitting next to her.

"I'll talk to anyone helping that girl. I thought I was messed up until I saw her." She shivered as Colin walked past her to sit by me. "I guess someone just walked across my grave." I shooed Colin away from us. He sulked as he walked away, but he knew some non-Survivors were able to sense him, usually those who also sensed ghosts.

"Messed up how?" I asked.

"She was real scared. Said her husband was going to find her. I tried to tell her she was safe. But I guess we were wrong. Is she safe now?"

"She is as safe as can be for a woman in a coma. Her hospital room is secure and she even has a pastor that watches over her."

"She needs that. Someone looking out for her." She frowned. "I tried you know."

"I know, sometimes these things are out of our hands. Do you know who her husband is?"

"Nah, she never even told me his name. She said she didn't want to put me in danger."

"Did she have a picture of him?"

"How many people do you know that keep pictures of their abuser in their wallet?"

"Point taken."

"I thought I saw him, once, but I can't be sure."

"What did you see?"

"We had gone into town to get some supplies. We were almost through the register when she turned her back to the front windows of the store and asked me to hurry. Then she asked the clerk if there was a back way out. I tried to figure out who had spooked her but there were several men in front of the store. About the only thing they had in common was that they were all white. A few days later she asked me to look after her kid if she didn't make it back and she hiked out to the road to catch a bus to town. I never saw her again."

Colin howled and pointed his nose at one of the children playing in the yard. It was a young boy wearing a baseball jersey and ball cap on his head.

"Is that her son?" I asked pointing him out.

"No, that isn't her son," she said.

I could tell she was telling the truth, but I felt her fear wash over me. I felt my body itching to run. "I wouldn't put anyone here in any danger." I couldn't figure out why Colin thought the boy was important. There wasn't much else that Laura could tell me that would let us identify her. I thanked her for her time and she went to get Mary to drive me home. While I was waiting I went to the playground and asked several children what their mother's names were. The universal answer was "Mommy". I gave up and walked over to the car where Colin was waiting for me. He had finished going through the house and property already. Mary took Colin, whom she still couldn't see, and me back to the park.

I heard the chatter of the crowd before I saw anyone, as I walked up the side street of the bakery. A large crowd had formed in and around the Wonderland Bakery. I put my face on the window and scanned the crowd. At first, I only saw regular customers, but after the crowd repositioned a gap formed in the center of the room and I saw a tall man using a video camera at the front of the store.

I heard a deep laugh that pulled me away from the window. I saw Colin's back as he was talking to three men, two of which I had seen as the protestors at the pub. When I got closer, I recognized the third as Tom.

Claire. I heard Tom's voice echo in my mind so loudly that I jumped. *Don't say anything. Just get him out of here. They're looking for an excuse for violence while the camera crew is here.*

"I don't know you look awfully familiar," Collin said to Tom rubbing his chin.

"What's with all the yelling?" I asked.

"This 'man' is attempting to take our freedom of speech away," the taller protestor said.

"Well that doesn't seem very nice. You should leave."

"What?" Colin's smile turned to a frown.

"Now." Colin grunted but then walked to the bakery.

"I'm sorry he bothered you nice folks," I said.

Thank you, Tom said in my mind. I thought, *You're welcome.*

I walked into Wonderland Bakery. After some maneuvering, I made it to the front of the crowd, where Colin was standing. I elbowed him and told him he couldn't blow someone's cover just because he didn't like them.

"Being able to experience your wildest fantasies from the safety of your bed," the interviewer, Katie, said. "I can't think of anyone who wouldn't want that." From reading her mind, she was thinking of Matt Damon in a cowboy outfit.

"Thank you for sharing your story with us. You're brave to be willing to come forward. I know the public hasn't been welcoming to the Survivors, but I for one find you a blessing not a curse," Katie smiled.

"Thank you for giving me a chance to share my bakery with you." Alice handed her a cellophane wrapped cookie. "I'd like you to be my first official customer."

Katie took the sugar cookie. "Thank you, Alice. I'm

honored to be your first customer. Come down to Wonderland Bakery and try out this magical cookie for yourself. This wraps up this evening's "Survivor Story". Join us tomorrow for a look at a man who can talk to horses. If we're lucky, he just might be able to give us an inside tip to tomorrow night's horse race." Katie's smile disappeared when the camera turned off and she rubbed her cheeks.

After Katie and her crew left, a long line formed to buy Alice's cookies. Our spot started a block away from the bakery and we were nowhere near the end of the line. When it was our turn to be served Alice leaned over the counter and gave me a hug.

"Did you see it?" Alice asked as she started boxing all the cookies Colin pointed at.

"Yes, but just the end because we were delayed." I glared at Colin and then turned back to Alice. "You were great on camera." She handed me the box of cookies and I handed her some money. We took the cookies and a couple of drinks to a table by the front door.

"Why were you pointing to that little boy?"

"It wasn't a boy," Colin mumbled with a mouth full of cookie.

"Ok, I'll just wait until you're done with your cookies. There is no use talking to you when you're hungry."

After 2 cookies and a long drink of milk, Colin repeated, "It wasn't a boy."

"Whatever, I'm not interested in the child's gender. I want to know why you got so excited and kept pointing at him or her as the case may be."

"I smelled Susanna Russo on her and none of the other children."

"Could he have just borrowed his clothes or something else from Susanna's child or be the child of her roommate?

"SHE could have, but I thought you should have taken a closer look and checked her out."

Colin left after he had polished off his cookies and a

couple of mine. I looked at my watch; it was past eight, which told me Officer Olsson had started his night shift. I was in no hurry to go back to the apartment. I watched the crowd and was surprised by the support. Not one customer had a bad thought about Alice or her gift. Maybe she was right; we needed more Survivors showing the benefits of the Survivor side-effects to lessen the fear.

When I started feeling tired enough to sleep, I headed back to the apartment.

The apartment was quiet, so I tried to quietly pass through the kitchen to my bedroom. Out of the corner of my eye I saw Trevor standing at the living room window, with the curtains pulled. When I walked closer I saw he held the curtains open just enough to peek out.

"What are you doing?" I asked. Trevor closed the curtains and turned in my direction. I sucked in a breath of air to keep from gasping at his appearance. His pale white face had the beginnings of a scruffy beard and he had black circles under his eyes that match his retro glasses. By the stains on his outfit and the smell of onions and well-aged cheese that grew stronger with his movement, I knew he hadn't taken a bath. His lack of hygiene wasn't what worried me the most, it was his eyes. Ever since I've known him his eyes moved rapidly and had a gleam that made me think he was up to something. Now, they seemed as dull and lifeless as a doll's eyes.

Trevor went back to looking out the window. I pulled him away from the curtain and shook him. "Trevor."

"Claire?" Something inside of Trevor turned on because he was now looking at me. "Is something wrong?"

"No. What are you looking at?"

"Protestors. They've been out since this morning," Trevor said.

I opened the curtains and scanned the view. He was right; the protestors were still in front of the bakery. "Poor Alice," I said pulling back from the curtains. "I saw them in front of the store."

"They're here because of her?"

"She went public with the bakery."

"How could you let her do that? This is going to end badly."

"I couldn't stop her from doing this any more than I could stop you from going public."

"I never thought it'd turn out like this. I want to help the Survivors who are suffering from what I did."

"It wasn't your fault, if you didn't do it someone else would have figured it out. At this point, I think only time will bring people around."

"Thanks. I know you haven't been my biggest fan. I just can't watch my friends die, while I'm being protected."

"You could always help."

"How? I'm locked away from the world."

"Why not make me a list of all your friends and everyone that worked with you on your research? It might help keep them safe, might even help me find who hurt Mrs. Cooper."

"I can do that. I'll go work on it now." He bent down and gave me a hug, I held my breath.

"You might want to take a bath first." I picked a Cheeto off the sleeves of his robe.

"Yeah, I thought I smelled something. I was hoping it was the cop." He nodded toward Officer Olsson. I almost missed it but I caught a small smile flash on his face as he made his way to his bedroom.

THE PUZZLE KEEPER

CHAPTER SEVEN

Tom was sitting at Colin's desk rummaging through his desk drawers, when I got into the office the next day. I sat down at my desk and started going through my email.

"Aren't you going to say anything?" Tom asked.

"Good morning, Tom. It's so good to see you," I said without looking up.

"You've got nothing else to say?"

"Not unless you start going through my stuff." I looked up and Tom shook his head before going back to tinkering with Colin's desk.

I was in the middle of reading the file Austin had sent me on the Cooper case, when Colin came into the office. "Morning," he said cheerfully. He was wearing the same shirt he was wearing last night and smelled vaguely of roses.

"Afternoon," I corrected him.

"I guess it is." He sat down in his chair and turned on his computer. When he tried to move the mouse it wouldn't budge. He used both hands and tried to rip it off but the force of his pull toppled the screws Tom loosened in his chair and he fell backwards. "TOM!"

"What's the matter?" I asked trying hard to keep the laughter to a minimum.

"Look at this?" He tried to lift every item on his desk and it wouldn't budge. "What else did he do?" He asked himself.

"You rang?" Tom asked leaning on the frame of our office door.

"What did you do?" Colin asked.

"You mean with the drawers?" Tom asked.

"The drawers?" He pulled out the drawers in his desk. The drawers were empty except for a picture of Tom standing in front of Colin's files and possessions. "Where's my stuff?"

"You'll get it back when you've apologized to my satisfaction," Tom said with a smirk.

"Apologize?! What makes you think I'm going to apologize?"

"I'm assuming you are attached to the contents of your desk."

"Well, since I can't work without my files, I'll just tell Gail. I don't think she'll be pleased."

"What I did will add a reprimand to my file, what you did will get you fired. You're lucky, I took your things and didn't go to Gail."

"There is way too much testosterone in this room. I'm done with this. I don't want to be in the middle of whatever dysfunctional relationship you two have anymore. I'm tired of being collateral damage. I've never done anything to either of you and yet I get pulled in every time."

Colin started to say something but I held up my hand and said, "I don't want to hear it ... Both of you go figure this out in Tom's office."

They both looked stunned but complied and left my office. I didn't hear any shouting so I assumed they were patching things up and went back to reviewing the new information.

Colin came back about an hour later with his stuff. After he had put everything away, I went over all the information Austin had sent us on the progress they made on the Cooper case. Unfortunately, there was nothing useful in the new information. The lab didn't find any physical evidence to tie anyone to the crime. It became clear that we needed to find answers from Nadine. We decided our next move should be interviewing the aunt again at the Coopers' house. We hoped that being at the crime scene would trigger her to think about what happened the day of the crime.

We arranged to meet the family at the mansion, the next day at roughly the same time of day as the murder. They were standing outside the mansion when we arrived.

"I know you're all wondering why you're here," Colin said.

"None of us killed her," Mike said.

"We didn't say anyone here did," I added.

"We're hoping that one of you will remember something that happened that day that was out of the ordinary that could lead us to the killer. Something small that didn't seem important at the time."

"What could we possibly know?" Mike asked.

"Well, we need to know how the killer got access to the house. There were no signs of a break-in so either someone let him into the house or he had a key," Colin said.

As soon as Colin mentioned the key, I felt guilt emanating from Russ and he glanced at the rocks lining the path to the house. Colin caught that look too and moved toward the rocks. Now Russ was starting to panic. I nodded at Colin and he picked up the rock he was standing next to.

"Ah, I think I see how the killer got access to the house," Colin said as he took a key from inside the rock. "Mr. Cooper, how many people know about this rock?"

I was getting shock from Mr. Cooper. It was clear even he didn't know about the rock.

Russ blushed and said, "No one but me knows about the rock. Dad, I'm sorry but you said I'd lose computer privileges if I lost my key one more time." He started to tear up and Mr. Cooper put his arm around his shoulders.

"The killer would have found a way to get in no matter what. This isn't your fault," I said.

"Mr. Cooper, why don't you and Russ stay here?

Nadine and Mike can take us through the house," Colin said.

I could sense reluctance from both Mike and Nadine but for different reasons. Nadine did not want to relive her sister's death while Mike thought this was a waste of good drinking time.

While we went through the house Colin continued to ask them questions about the house and their actions on the day of the murder. Neither of them had any revealing thoughts as we went through the downstairs. As we approached the master bedroom Nadine, Colin and I dreaded going in but Mike was curious. He stepped through the door almost eagerly. He bent over the bed and said, "Wow, is this where it happened?" I wasn't picking up any guilt from him but Nadine was practically incoherent with fear as she looked in and saw him bending over the bed. The scene in her mind was the same scene except with Mike bending over her sister's body. She backed out of the doorway and refused to come any farther. I put my hand on her arm and my mind was flooded with images of the crime scene but then I got images that didn't make any sense. There were many scenes flashing through her mind, so fast it was hard for me to focus. The ones that came through most clearly were a street sign, Bello Road. Then an old brick building with two large barrels standing in front of an old door. She walked down a dirt trail in the woods to a large body of water surrounded by oak trees. Nadine pulled away from me and the images stopped. I turned from Nadine to Mike to see if he was thinking about how he killed Mrs. Cooper but Mike was back to thinking about how he would rather be at the bar with his buddies. He had to be the most callous killer I had ever encountered.

CHAPTER EIGHT

The next morning, I woke up at my computer desk. My neck and shoulders felt stiff like rusted hinges, but I didn't want to move. With the warm sun that lit up the room, and sounds of traffic coming through the window, life seemed ordinary again. For just a moment I could pretend it was all dream.

"Claire?" Molly asked. I opened my eyes enough to see Molly at the doorway. "I hate to wake you but you're going to be late for work."

"I'm up." I lifted my face off the computer desk. I rubbed my cheek and could feel the marks left by the keyboard on the right side of my face.

"You do know your bed is only a few feet away," Molly said. "You only had to walk a few steps."

"Thanks for the tip. I don't even remember falling asleep." I stretched my arms, and a blanket draped around my neck fell to the floor. I looked at the purple fleece blanket and then at Molly. "Thank you."

"I couldn't let you freeze." Her cheeks blushed. "Go take a shower. I'll make you some breakfast."

I could smell sausage sizzling on the stove when I got out of the shower. I threw on a pair of black slacks and red blouse, and ran to the kitchen. I took a seat at the table across from Officer Myers and Trevor.

"It smells really good, dear," Trevor said over sounds of

the sausage and hash browns, Molly was cooking in the kitchen.

"Thank you, Honey," Molly said.

"What took you so long, Claire? Molly wouldn't start breakfast until you got up. Some of us are withering away here." Trevor patted his tummy. Oddly, although Trevor was thin, he had a small paunch.

"Some of us are still working," I said.

Molly came out with a plate full of sausage and another with hash browns, and put them next to a stack of pancakes that were already on the table. We all looked at Molly. She smiled and said, "Go ahead."

We all took turns passing around the dishes of food. "Still working on the Cooper case?" Trevor asked.

"That's what I was working on last night when I fell asleep at the computer," I said.

"Do you have any leads?" Trevor asked.

"We don't have any real leads; except for the images I pulled out of the mind of a woman I think helped cover up the crime." I ate a bite of my apple pancakes and they were luscious as usual. "But even that isn't helpful. I can't figure out where the images come from. Or even why it's important."

"I know the area pretty well," Officer Myers said. "I have only been out of patrol for a year."

"Any help would be wonderful." I went and retrieved my work notebook from my briefcase and handed it to Officer Myers.

"This is out my patrol area, but I've done some hiking in these mountains. I don't recognize the description of this building, but I think I know the sign. You only saw half of it, it's not "bello", it's Montebello Road. It's up in the mountains."

"Thank you," I said. "That will help narrow down the area."

"Not by much," Officer Myers said. "It's a huge area. The street itself is long and winds through the mountains.

There are also hiking trails that run several miles through the woods and a park with the same name."

"It's a start. I have a teenage boy who needs to know who killed his mother. I'm willing to do anything to make that happen even if it means I need to hike through the entire area myself," I said.

After breakfast I felt re-energized now that I was fed and had a general location to search.

Colin was already at his desk when I reached the office. He was entirely too happy, grinning for no apparent reason, plus his hair was neat and he had shaved: all the classic signs that he had had a good date last night.

"I was starting to get worried," he said.

"Overslept," I said.

"Did you find anything?" Colin asked.

"Yeah. After searching all night for anything named Bello, Officer Myers told me over breakfast that it's probably Montebello Road."

"That's great. I knew you'd figure it out," Colin said.

"You could have figured it out too," I said. As I sat down I realized that I had two different socks on my feet.

"How can I help you when I didn't experience it?" Colin smiled.

"Uh huh. You don't fool me. I bet you had a date with your dad's new waitress," I said pulling out the aspirin bottle in my desk drawer and popping two in my mouth. "It's not like you need to see the images to try and find the street name."

I looked at Colin, maybe I said more than I should have. I didn't mind doing the work. I just didn't like how smug he was. He got to go out and have fun while I had to do all the work.

"Should we go now?" He asked.

"I wish it was that easy. The name is connected to a long road, hiking trails and a park. It's too much to just go out and explore."

"I see. Maybe I can help you with that later." He pulled

out a yellow envelope from his desk drawer. "In the meantime, I picked up some photos of Nadine and Mike from Mr. Cooper. I thought we could go check out alibis."

"Oh good, let's start with Nadine."

On the way down to the parking lot, Colin offered to drive. It wasn't really an offer. He hasn't let me drive us anywhere since I drove in a snowstorm up in Seattle. I learned the hard way why you should drive slower than the speed limit when black ice might be on the road. Though in my defense, they shouldn't call it black ice, when in fact the ice is clear and impossible to see."

We stopped first at the gas station. Unfortunately, their security camera had already overwritten the footage from the night in question. We were hoping we had better luck at Target.

"Excuse me; do you know where the manager is?" I asked the security guard that stood near the cash registers just inside Target. He didn't look much older than a high school senior.

"Is there something I can help you with, Ma'am?" He smiled at me, showing his braces.

"No, we just need to talk to the manager," Colin said.

The security guard didn't even look his way but simply told me, "That'd be Mr. Murphy. I think he's in the electronic section right now."

"Thank you," I said with a smile.

"I do what I can for a pretty lady," he said. I giggled as I caught Colin rolling his eyes.

The manager was helping a woman stack a variety of classic movies on the shelf.

"Do you need help finding something?" The manager asked picking up a stack of, *Casablanca* DVDs from a box on the floor.

"Are you the manager?" Colin asked.

"Yes. How can I help you?" He put the DVDs he was holding on the shelf and turned around.

"I'm Agent Colin O'Connor and this is my partner

Agent Bennett. We were hoping to ask you a few questions," Colin said. We both showed him our badges. The woman next to the manager stood up empty handed from the cardboard box to see the badges.

"Go back to work, Donna," the manager said. "I'm Paul, is something the matter?" He looked at the badges. "We don't discriminate against Survivors. We have four employees that are Survivors." I noticed the woman was now casually rifling through the box of DVDs. I could tell by her thoughts that Paul hadn't shared with his employees that four Survivors worked there. She didn't seem to want to hurt them, just had a general need for gossip.

"Everything is fine." I indicated my head towards Donna. "Could we talk in private?"

"Of course," he said. He led us to his office at the front of the store. After he closed the door he asked. "What do you two need?"

"We are investigating a murder that happened a few nights ago, up in the hills," Colin said.

"I think I heard about that. The lady that was stabbed to death?" Paul asked.

"Yes, that's the one," I said.

"What a shame. Mrs. Cooper was one of a kind. She set up donation drives here a few times." He looked at us. "I'll do everything I can to help you solve her murder."

"Thank you," I said. I handed Paul the pictures of Nadine and Mike.

"I don't know him, but we all know her," Paul said with a sigh.

"Nadine is Mrs. Cooper's sister," I said.

"No, really?! I can't imagine two more different women. Mrs. Cooper was a real lady, kind and generous to everyone she met. Her sister on the other hand … well, I shouldn't gossip," Paul said.

"We need to verify that Nadine came to the store on the day of the murder," Colin said.

"So you're hoping we have a security tape with her on

it?" Paul asked.

"Yes, preferably showing when she arrived and when she left," Colin said.

"I'll get you the tapes for the entrances and the cashiers," Paul said.

Paul left the room and came back with a laptop. He set up the video on it, and excused himself to take care of an emergency in the toy department. It wasn't a long search since we knew from the receipt she gave the police that she bought her items at 4:50. Once we spotted Nadine, Colin changed the speed of the video to slow motion. We watched as the cashier scanned the items. A few moments later, the cashier started to pick something up, and stopped when Nadine started moving around and dramatically motioning with her arms. She moved around enough that we couldn't see what she was buying. Soon as she was done paying she left in a hurry with her items glued to her side. Her behavior was so strange that it made us even more curious.

"Did that help at all?" Paul asked, poking his head into the room.

"Maybe, but we need to talk to the cashier," Colin said pointing to the woman on the screen.

"Sure," Paul played the tape again watching the woman's face. "That's Kim. To be honest with you, even with Nadine being as memorable as she is, I'm not sure how much Kim will remember, it's been several days," Paul said.

"It's worth a shot. When does she start her shift?" I asked.

Paul looked at a piece of paper on the wall. "Not for another three hours."

"Thanks, we will come back then," Colin said.

The Target was too far away for us to drive back and forth. Instead, I bought some maps of the area and we went to a coffee shop to have a snack to kill time.

I recognized Kim when we walked back into Target. She was already at a cash register with a long line of customers in her lane. Kim didn't even notice us when we stopped in front of her.

"Kim?" Colin asked.

"Yeah?" She asked continuing to scan items.

"We're Agent O'Connor and Bennett." She looked our way and we showed our badges. "We have a couple of questions if you have time."

"Paul said you two were coming," Kim said. "I can't leave my register until my break, but I can answer a couple of questions while I work."

"On Sunday, this woman came into Target," I said showing her the picture of Nadine.

"Yeah, we all know her. She's hard to forget. That night she was worse than usual; she threw a big fit in my lane," Kim said.

"Why?" Colin asked.

"She wanted to pay with cash for some of her items. She didn't tell me that was what she wanted, she just started freaking out," Kim said handing a bag to an elderly man and starting to scan items for the next customer.

"What items did she want to pay cash for?" I asked.

"That was the weird part. I see people pay with cash for some of their items all the time, but normally it's for gifts or something embarrassing that they want on a separate receipt or something they buy last minute after everything else has been rung up. But Nadine bought a shovel and a lighter with the cash." Kim stopped bagging and looked at us. "That's odd isn't it?"

"Yes, very odd indeed," I said. We thanked her for her time and warned her that a detective might call to question her.

When we got to the car, I called Austin and let him know what we had found at Target. After I hung up, Colin asked, "Do you think she buried or burned what she took from the crime scene?"

"I don't know. The only thing that matters is finding out where she went after Target, and hoping she was dumb enough to bury it."

"It's going to have to wait until tomorrow," he said. "The area is too big to search randomly. I'll drop you at work to get your car and we can meet at the pub to look over the maps."

CHAPTER NINE

For a few brief minutes driving from work to the Red Lion pub, I had the pleasure of complete and utter silence. Every few miles the neighborhood style and décor changed by decade. I started by driving past blocks of 1950's style homes with whacky mailboxes, and ended by driving by chic modern homes with edgy exteriors. After parking the car at home, I walked to the pub.

Colin had gotten us a quiet booth in the back. He was smiling and watching, Brittany serving tables nearby. His smile went away when I put the stack of maps and travel guides on the table.

From the way Brittany flirted with Colin as she approached our table, it confirmed my suspicions that she was responsible for Colin's less than full attention on our case. We ordered two burgers, some fries and two coffees. Colin refused to do any work until he was fed, so I stuck my stack of maps and travel guides on the seat next to me.

Brittany came to our table as we started slowing down on our burgers. "I just wanted to let you know, that I'm done with my shift. If you want anything else you will have to ask Gene." She pointed to a young man picking up a tray of drinks from the bar.

"Off your shift already?" Colin asked. "Do you want to join us?"

"Sure. If you don't mind," she said.

"I mind," I said staring straight at Colin and ignoring Brittany. "You already promised me you'd help with the maps since you didn't last night."

"Come on Claire. I can help with her here. Maybe she could help," Colin said.

"No, because I know how this works. You both flirt, and I end up doing the work," I said.

"I'll go I didn't want to intrude. I just thought." Brittany whined on the verge of tears.

"You can join us," Colin said patting her arm.

"Oh, thank you," Brittany sat next to him.

I handed him a map from my stack and I picked up another map.

He had just unfolded the map when Brittany asked, "What are you looking for?"

"It's for a case. I'd tell you about it but it's confidential," Colin said.

"Oh that is exciting." She stroked his arm and then pointed to the map. "That's a nice spot to look at the stars. It's near my apartment."

"You'll have to show me sometime." Colin grinned. He was so focused on Brittany that he completely missed the glare I directed toward him.

"I'd love to tonight; my roommate is out for the next few nights. If you weren't busy working on your case, that is," she said.

"That does sound nice," Colin said.

"It's a shame," I said. "How do you think we should start looking at buildings near the road or hiking trial?"

"It's nice, I even have a hot tub," Brittany said.

"Really?" Colin laid down his map on the table.

"So this is how it's going to go? Another night I stay up working, and you just ditch me for a girl you'll only play with for a few weeks?" I asked.

He was still chatting with Brittany. I took my coffee and the stack of maps to the bar. Sean came by and placed a basket of chips in front of me.

"What'cha doin' lass?" I looked up from my map. Sean was trying to fit his large stubby fingers wrapped in a dishtowel to dry the inside of a bar glass.

"I'm working on a case. I need to find a location based on a few landmarks."

"Why isn't the lad helpin'?" He nodded at his son and then smiled. "Ah I see. Well maybe I can help. I know I'm just an old man. But still got the wits about me."

"Any help would be appreciated. I just really want to solve this one," I said. "Do you know of any antique brick buildings, with large barrels in front of it on or near Montebello Road?"

After taking a sip of whiskey, he said, "I know of an old winery, name Pichetti, I think. It's pretty far up in the mountains on Montebello Road."

"Are you sure? This area is crawling with vineyards and wineries," I said.

"Lass, you think I don't know every pub, winery and drinkin' hole in this town? Even if I didn't, this one's special. They made it a landmark. Oldest in the area."

"Thank you," I kissed him on the cheek.

"Anythin' for you lass," he said with a smile.

I laid down the map in front of Colin. "I hope you got a good scent off of Nadine."

"Why?" he took his arm off Brittany shoulder. Brittany looked up at me her lower lip sticking out and her eyes narrowed.

"It's time to go hunting," I said and winked at her.

CHAPTER TEN

"Let me get this straight, it's the middle of the night and we're going to go on a hike to find something buried in the dirt in the middle of the woods?" Colin asked.

"That sounds about right, though technically, it's not the middle of the night. We've got a good hour before the sun sets. It's the middle of summer after all," I said taking a long sip of my coffee and letting the tingling warmth swirl in my mouth.

"You're splitting hairs. It's getting dark. It'd be easier and safer if we did this in the morning," Colin said.

"Thanks for the tip. I don't want to take the chance that Nadine will come back to move or destroy what she took from the crime scene," I said.

"She doesn't seem smart enough for that."

"She was smart enough to bury the evidence in the woods or destroy it. I just don't want to take the chance."

"Good point," Colin said. We rode in silence, while I scanned the trees.

"Stop!" I said, and Colin hit the brakes in the middle of the road.

"What?"

"This is the place."

"Did you have to do that?"

"Sorry," I muffled a laugh. "I'm just excited."

"I'm sure you are," Colin said parking the car in the

empty parking lot.

I recognized the building immediately from the image I pulled from Nadine's head. The buildings in the area dated back to the 1800's. We passed the two barrels and knocked on the old wooden door.

An older man with a graying goatee opened the door. "What?"

"I'm Agent Bennett and this is my partner Agent O'Connor," I said and we showed him our badges. "We talked on the phone."

"Yeah, come in." He picked up a map and a flashlight from behind the counter. "What's so important on the trail it couldn't wait till morning?" He asked.

"It's part of an open investigation. We can't really talk about it," Colin said.

"That figures," he said.

"Is there anywhere around here that someone could privately build a fire?" I asked.

"Fire!? What are you two planning? There are no fires allowed in this park at all with the fire danger as high as it is in the summer," he said.

"We aren't planning anything, we were just wondering if anyone could have a fire here without anyone knowing," Colin said.

"It'd have to be small and smokeless not to be noticed when fires are not allowed," he said.

He handed us a map of the trail and a flashlight. "I ain't going to wait around till you get back."

"We understand," Colin said.

"Thank you for opening the trails to us," I said as we walked out of the winery.

"Give me a minute," Colin said. I went to the large gate that led to the trail. I fell backwards on to a rock, when I caught something moving behind me. I stumbled to my feet, and saw a wolf leap towards me from the side of the woods. The dying light of the sun and the cover of the trees made the wolf look more substantial.

"Not funny," I said to Colin. Colin tilted his nose down and looked up at me.

"Ha!" I continued to grumble for a few more minutes about his lack of consideration.

"Is your body safe here?" I glanced over to his car, its windows were well tinted, but I knew Colin's body was slumped in there. He bobbed his head. "The pond is part of the trail. It's pretty far in."

I followed Colin as he trotted along the dirt trail, his nose smelling the ground and the air. We must have walked a few miles before Colin froze where another trail split off from ours leading into a patch of oak trees. Before I could ask if he smelled anything he started running into the woods.

"I'm not as fast as you," I said turning on the flashlight. I could barely see the gaps between the oak trees. Jagged branches stung my arms as I whipped passed them. He stopped. I nearly fell over trying to stop with him. "Why did you stop?" He nodded his head forward. I lifted the flashlight, and saw the muddy pond. Colin put his nose to the ground and walked slowly around the rim of the pond. He pawed the dirt, under a fallen tree. I bent down and felt the ground. The dirt was loose and crumbled in my hand unlike the rest of the dirt around it, which was hard as clay.

"I'll call. You go back to your body and lead them here." Before I could finish the sentence he was gone. After calling Austin, I sat down in the cold wet dirt, and waited.

"What are we digging up?" Detective Moseley asked as we watched Austin use a small shovel to dig in the loose dirt.

"No clue. I just know it's important," Colin said.

"How, exactly, did you know where to look?" Detective Mosley asked. I didn't really know what to say. I didn't feel comfortable sharing our secrets with Detective Moseley yet and there wasn't a logical excuse to finding the spot in the middle of the woods.

"Found something," Austin said. I took a deep breath in, thank God for a distraction. Austin used a gloved hand to pick up a plastic Target shopping bag. "Well you're right about one thing," Austin said looking into the bag. "This looks to be important for our case." He pulled out a bloody knife which he put in an evidence bag. After that he pulled a small decorative pillow from the bag, with the initials, EC on the front.

"This appears to be the pillow that Mrs. Cooper was smothered with," he said, pointing to marks in the pillow that look like bite marks, where stuffing was still popping out. It was also missing a blue ribbon.

"I guess it's time to look over their alibis again for any holes." Detective Moseley grunted. "Just how I was hoping to spend my evening."

"We will call you when we have enough evidence to bring them in again," Austin said.

CHAPTER ELEVEN

As I walked into the apartment I could see Trevor still glued to the window. It didn't look like he'd moved since I had left this morning. I turned to Officer Olsson and asked, "Has he been at the window all day?"

"I only took over an hour ago so I can only say that he has been there since I got here," Officer Olsson said.

"Trevor, how are you doing?" I asked.

"Claire, I'm so glad you're home! Officer Olsson won't listen to me but I know you will."

"Listen to what, Trevor?" I asked.

"He keeps saying that there are people out there but when I look out the window there isn't anyone there. I'm thinking maybe it's cabin fever, if you know what I mean."

"No, it's not cabin fever, there are people out there sneaking into Alice's bakery. Look, there's one now."

I went to the window but I couldn't see anyone. "Trevor, maybe you should come away from the window. There isn't anyone there."

"Yes, there is. They slipped around the corner. I'll prove it to you. Just keep watching."

"In a few minutes. I'll be right back," I said as I slipped out of the room to call Molly privately.

While I was waiting for Molly to come to the nurses' station, I looked out my bedroom window. I could hear Molly come on the line as I said "Son of a bitch" and hung up. There was Trevor in the alley.

As I got to the living room, Officer Olsson was coming out of the bathroom. "How could you let Trevor leave the apartment?"

"What do you mean leave?" He asked.

"I saw him in the alley" as I jerked the front door open and ran to the elevator. I could hear Officer Olsson following me muttering obscenities. Officer Olsson reported "the breach" while we rode down in the elevator. We dashed out of the elevator when we reached the ground floor and couldn't see Trevor in any direction.

"Let's try the bakery," He said.

As we rounded the corner, we saw Trevor with his face pressed up against the glass.

"Oh, good, you're here," Trevor said.

"Come along, let's go back, Dr. Harris," Officer Olsson said in a soothing voice.

"We're already here. Let's go in and make sure Alice is ok," Trevor said.

"And then, you'll go back to the apartment?" I asked.

"No, we need to go back now," Officer Olsson said.

While the officer and I looked at each other ready to argue our point, Trevor ran around the corner of the building. We had no choice but to follow him.

We caught up with him as he reached the back door of the bakery and started to pull the door open. Officer Olsson grabbed his arm. "You can't go in there"

Just then, we heard the sound of breaking glass. Officer Olsson pulled his gun and motioned us to back up. I know he wanted us to wait in the alley but we crept behind him into the bakery anyway. The kitchen was empty but we could hear sounds coming from the break room. Officer Olsson approached it slowly and opened the door. His shoulders slumped and he holstered his weapon. Peeking around him, we could see Alice, Sean and a few of the other shop owners sitting around a table playing poker. One of them was sweeping up a broken mug that had fallen or been dropped.

"Really, Officer, this is just a friendly game, completely legal," Alice said. "No need for guns here"

"Sorry, ma'am, we had a complaint of suspicious persons lurking around the bakery," replied Officer Olsson as he glared at Trevor. "I guess someone had an overactive imagination."

"No problem, Officer. I'd rather have you check out reports of suspicious activity than ignore them when it's a real problem."

The three of us nodded to the poker players and took our leave. When we got to the alley, we met two more officers who had come as backup. Officer Olsson asked me to take Trevor upstairs while he explained to his fellow policemen. He didn't look happy. I imagined he would take a lot of ribbing for this incident of dangerous poker play.

Officer Olsson was plenty cranky by the time he came back to the apartment. "I hope you're happy," he told Trevor, "because of this incident, we will have to move you."

"Why, no one dangerous saw me," he said.

"You may feel that the poker players are safe but we can't control who they tell about your whereabouts plus I had to announce your description and location over the radio."

THE PUZZLE KEEPER

CHAPTER TWELVE

Austin called two days later to inform us that they found plenty of evidence to convict Nadine but nothing concrete to tie Mike to the crime. I knew he was guilty; I saw him do it. But visions from a telepath wouldn't hold up in court like a real eyewitness. After some persuasion Austin agreed to interview Mike again, this time with me in the room. I was hoping that Mike would think about the crime and lead me to some hard evidence.

We found the detectives at one of the many computer desks that cluttered the homicide department.

"Thanks for doing this," I said.

"No problem. I'm not convinced that Mike had anything to do with the crime, but since we need to interview Nadine again anyway, we might as well talk to Mike, too," Austin said.

"Do you have anything on Mike?" Colin asked.

"Only this. We found them in Mike's truck." Austin pulled out a small bundle of pamphlets from a portfolio and put them on the desk. I picked it up and read the first page, which was a meeting schedule for the Brotherhood of Humanity group. "It might point to motive but without a confession or some strong evidence Mike won't be arrested for the murder."

Colin agreed to sit in with Detective Moseley for the interview with Nadine so I could interview Mike with

Austin. I followed Austin into interrogation room A. The room was small; the size of a bathroom, containing only a small rectangular table and three chairs.

"How are you today, Mike?" Austin asked in a friendly voice, as we took seats around the table.

"Well I'm here, so not great," Mike said.

"Don't worry too much. We're just here to clear some things up," Austin said.

"Before we start, I'd like to put my hand on your wrist to check your pulse during this conversation." It was the only excuse I could think of to touch his skin. I needed the contact to help me focus on Mike and tune Austin's thoughts out.

"What like a lie detector?" Mike asked.

"Yes," I said and he put his arm out so I could lightly place my fingers on his wrist.

"Where were you the day that Mrs. Cooper was murdered?" Austin asked.

"How many times do I need to say it before you write it down?"

"We need to hear it again," Austin said with a stiff face. "Unless, of course, the problem is you can't remember what you said because it isn't true."

"Whoa, take it easy," Mike said. "I'll tell you again. I work as a handyman at my brother-in-law's apartment complexes. I was there all day."

"When did you leave?" Colin asked.

"I can't remember but it had to be late. I got home after Brian and Russ." That might have been what Mike was saying but what he was thinking was: *they don't need to know I made a pit stop on the way home. God, no one would blame me for needing a little lovin' before I went home to the bony shrew.*

"Did you stop anywhere on the way home?" I asked.

"Uh no," Mike said jerking around in his chair. His thoughts grew frantic but only about being caught cheating.

"I think the lady you stopped to see would say something different," I said.

"The only 'lady' I saw my wife that night. I want to know what this is about right now or I'm walking." He pounded a finger on the desk and stared at Austin.

"All right Mike, I'm going to level with you. We know what happened. We know what you and your wife did to Mrs. Cooper," Austin said staring directly into Mike's eyes. "At this point we just want to know why."

"I don't know what you're talking about. We didn't do anything," He said. "Well I didn't do anything to her. Why would I?

"I know of at least one reason." Austin pulled out the small bundle of pamphlets from the portfolio and put them on the table. "You're involved with a known anti-Survivor group."

"Where did you get this?" Mike asked.

"We found it under the driver's seat in your truck, during our search last night," Austin said.

Mike flipped through the bundle of pamphlets from the Brotherhood of Humanity group. "What does this have to do with Eileen's death?"

"I'm glad you asked." Austin pulled out a piece of paper from the bottom of the pack. I noticed it was the same flyer of the *Twenty Most Dangerous Survivors* that I had seen at Mrs. Cooper's crime scene. "Because of this." He pointed to the picture of Mrs. Cooper.

"I don't get it." Mike shook his head. "She wasn't a Survivor."

"No, but she was a supporter of the Survivors," Austin said. "You must have been furious to learn about Russ and Mrs. Cooper's secret involvement in the research. It'd be understandable if you felt you needed to expose their support."

He shook his head. "It's not what it looks like. I didn't tell anyone about her fundraisers. I could care less about what she did."

"If you didn't care, why were you at the meeting?" I asked.

"I did go to the meeting but only for this girl that I'm seeing. She was all into this stuff, and well, I was into her."

"So there is another woman? What's her name?" Austin asked.

"Sandy something. She works at Old Timers, the country bar," Mike said.

"We'll check that out. See what she has to say about the meeting and your whereabouts on the day of the murder," Austin said.

"You won't tell my wife will you?"

"I think you need to focus on what you and your wife did to Mrs. Cooper first," Austin said.

"I didn't kill her. I swear it." I closed my eyes and focused on his thoughts. He kept repeating, *I don't understand. I didn't do it.*

"We found the knife your wife buried. It has fingerprints on them, Austin said.

"Can't be mine," Mike said.

"No, they're your wife's prints," Austin said.

"Then why are you bothering me?" Mike asked.

"We think you both did the crime. Mrs. Cooper was heavier and stronger than her sister. Do you really think your wife was able to pull it off by herself?"

"Well, no, I doubt she's even smart enough. But I didn't help her."

"Is that the story you're sticking with?" Austin asked.

"That's the truth." Mike pulled his hand away from mine. A loud knock came from the door. Austin stood up and poked his head into the hallway.

"Your wife has confessed to the crime. To both of you doing the crime," Austin said.

"No. I don't care what she said. She's lying." Mike pushed the small table; it nicked my knee before it slammed against the wall.

"You need to calm down or I'll have you restrained," Austin said. Mike didn't say anything, but just shook his head and started to pace the room.

"Mike, we have enough evidence to arrest both of you for the murder of Mrs. Cooper. You might want to think about telling us the truth. We might be able to help you if you do," Austin said.

"How can I? I didn't do it!"

"We can't help you without a real alibi or a confession. Just think about it. When you want to talk, I'll be ready to listen. Right now, an officer is on his way to take you to lock up," Austin said.

I started to leave the room. "Please, you got to believe me," Mike said.

THE PUZZLE KEEPER

CHAPTER THIRTEEN

The next morning when I walked into the office I found Colin and Tom in the middle of arguing over a newspaper. A small crowd of people hovered like nervous hummingbirds around them.

Tom interrupted me before I could ask what they were arguing about. "I guess you're feeling pretty good about yourselves right now."

"I'd say so." Colin puffed up his chest and handed me the paper. The Cooper case was featured in a large article in the newspaper, with a large picture of Colin with the detectives. "It's just great to feel recognized," Colin added in a mocking voice.

"Live it up. It won't last long. They might love you now. Just wait until you make a mistake. They'll turn on you," Tom said. I could feel the blood rushing away from my head, had we made a mistake in the Cooper case?

"I hope it does," Gail said from behind me. "This is the first piece of positive support for this agency. We need more in the media showing us working alongside non-survivors. For that reason, you two are going to be the official liaison for cases involving the Survivors in not only San Jose but the whole Santa Clara County. You'll be working alongside with Detective Hughes and Detective Moseley on all cases unless there is a reason you feel they're not qualified for that type of case." Gail paused and looked at us. We both shook our heads.

"Good. Now can we please get back to work," Gail's pudgy nose flared slightly in a sigh.

When we both sat back at our desks Colin asked, "What's going on? You didn't seem to happy about working with the detectives?"

"No, that's not it. I've just got a feeling we made a mistake," I said.

"How?" Colin asked. "We got prints. We got the weapon. We even got a confession. What more do we need?"

"I know all the evidence points to them doing it. It's just … Mike's thoughts didn't reveal anything that would make me think he did it."

"If you feel that strongly about it, we can take another look at it later. Quietly. You've got to promise me you won't tell anyone else about this. If you're wrong, you could ruin the case against them."

"I promise. I wouldn't do that to Russ. I don't want to be the cause him any more pain," I said. "It's probably nothing more than a bad feeling."

"Claire?" a male voice asked from the doorway to my office.

"About time you were back with lunch." I looked up and saw it was Austin not Colin.

"Oh, sorry," I said. "I thought you were someone else. Did we have a meeting set up?"

"Don't make me feel special or anything." He laughed. "No, we're stopping by for some follow up questions with Mr. Cooper and we thought we'd stop by."

"How are they doing?" I asked. Austin moved to the side to let Detective Moseley enter the room.

"It's hard to tell. You'd think getting the news of catching the murderer would make people happy, but it rarely happens that way. The news seems to hit them just as hard as when their loved one died.

I nodded. "Losing someone is hard. It's like

withdrawing from a drug. You're so used to having that person be there to give you that high. When they're gone you sink deep in misery. When you see their picture or smell their perfume you still get a jolt of high and it just starts over again."

"Is there a new case?" Colin asked walking into the room and putting a small wrapped burrito on my desk. By the smell of the burrito, it was chicken with one too many jalapeno peppers on top.

"Not yet," Detective Moseley said. "We have the next two days off. We haven't stopped except to sleep since we got the Cooper case."

"We will have our phones near us if anything happens," Austin said.

"We will try not to need you so you can get some rest," I said.

"Don't worry about it, I have given up on sleep since I became a detective," Austin said.

"Our boss tells us we're working together," Detective Moseley said.

"We are looking forward to working with both of you," Colin said.

"We are looking forward to it, too," Austin said.

Austin straightened his shirt and said something so fast it sounded like one long word in a foreign language. "Excuse me?" I asked.

"What about dinner tonight?" Austin asked. Detective Moseley politely pretended to be preoccupied with a file in his hand. "I mean since we are going to be working together it might be nice to get to know each other."

"You mean all four of us go out?" I asked.

"No I can't go, got plans with my kid." Detective Moseley winked dramatically at his partner.

"Thanks. Real subtle," Austin said.

"I try," Detective Moseley said with a grin.

"She can't." All three of us turned and looked at Colin. His face was unreadable.

"Excuse me?" I asked.

"We're having dinner tonight with Molly and Trevor," Colin said.

"He's right, I can't. I…" I started to say.

"It was just a thought," he interrupted, backing away from me. "I completely understand."

"No wait," I said. Austin turned around at the doorway. "My sister and her fiancé Trevor are moving out of my place tomorrow morning. I'm not going to see them for a while. I can go out tomorrow night."

"Tomorrow works. I will pick you up around seven?" He asked.

"I look forward to it," I wrote my address on the back of my business card and handed it to him.

"See you tomorrow," he said, putting the card in his pocket.

"Well?" Colin raised an eyebrow, after they left the room.

"What?" I asked.

"This is a bad idea." He glared at me. "You know what happens when you date normal guys."

"It's just dinner."

"It's a date," he said.

"Thanks for the clarification." I raised an eyebrow. "It hasn't been that long since I dated."

"So you want to date him?"

"I don't know what I want. I know he is a sweet guy. It's worth giving a chance to see if it works out."

"Until you tell him what you can do and he walks away."

"I don't think he would. He already thinks I'm a psychic because of those early cases we worked on together. A telepath isn't that much different." I shrugged at his comment. His eyes were narrow and I could see the muscles in his neck dancing. "I'm sorry, did you want to be invited?"

"It might have been nice," Colin said.

"Aren't you forgetting that you're having dinner tomorrow night with that redheaded waitress?"

He didn't say anything else so I went back to my paperwork. Colin hesitated a moment and then went back to playing solitaire.

CHAPTER FOURTEEN

Colin hitched a ride home with me after work. The streets surrounding my apartment were filled with moving trucks that blocked the lanes to the point where police officers had to guide traffic. Every time I had to stop the car, I thought of Molly. I was worried we would be late for Molly's dinner; she cleaned and cooked for this night for the last two evenings. When we walked into the apartment, I relaxed, at the sight of Officer Myers in the kitchen stirring a pot of gravy. "You're a brave man."

"What?" He asked.

"Don't bother, I tried to tell him." Trevor walked into the kitchen shaking his head.

"I'm just helping out," Office Myers said.

"There's a reason why you never see us helping Molly in the kitchen. It's a Jekyll and Hyde routine. She's all sweet until she gets into the kitchen," I said.

"Hey. I have gotten better about other people's lack of culinary skills," Molly said.

"Really? Because I distinctly remember Aunt Audrey running from the kitchen in tears last Christmas," I said.

"In my defense, I gave her a relatively easy task of whipping the cream, and she turned it into butter," Molly said.

"Well, she will never make that mistake again," I said walking into the kitchen. I gave her a hug and her wrinkled brow softened. "You know I tease because I care."

"Yeah, I know. But I have to say it's never a good idea to tease the cook. You never know what she might do to the food." She shook her head.

"Wise words," I said. "I'll behave until after dinner."

"Thanks for inviting me to dinner," Colin said embracing Molly. "Sorry we're late."

"I figured you'd be, traffic's been crazy all day," Molly said.

"Do you know who's moving?" I asked.

"I was only able to figure out two. The bad news is that Blissful Days Spa is moving. The good news is the couple across the street that raises parrots is also moving," Molly said.

"That's sad. It was nice to be in walking distance of a spa."

"Do you know why so many are moving?" Colin asked.

"I'm not entirely sure. I dropped in and talked to Alice this afternoon." Molly looked at the familiar pink box on the counter. "From what she has overheard, she thinks people are moving because of the bakery and pub. People seem to think this neighborhood is crawling with Survivors and people who support them.

"It might not be such a bad thing." Colin rubbed his chin. "If this place turns into a Survivor area, I might just have to move here."

I took a seat across from Trevor who was drinking a glass of merlot. "Do you want one?" He asked.

"After the week I have had, I could sure use one," I said.

"Bad day?" Trevor asked. He poured two glasses of wine and handed one to Colin and me.

"I wouldn't say that. After solving our first case, we got promoted to working as a permanent liaison to work with two local homicide detectives on Survivor crimes." I was about to share my concerns about the case, but Colin shook his head as if he was the telepath. "It can be draining dealing with these cases."

"I saw your case. It made the headlines this morning," Trevor said, picking up the newspaper page with the article on the Cooper case.

"It's going in the scrapbook," Molly said putting a large plate of potatoes down on the table next to a plate of slices of roast beef. "I'm so proud of you two."

"Why didn't they put your picture in the paper?" Trevor asked.

"I wasn't near them when they took it," I said.

"They couldn't have taken another picture?" Molly put her hands on her hip. "I bet you did more work than all of them put together." She looked at Colin. "You and Colin, that is."

"No, you're right. This case was all Claire," Colin said popping a few cheddar cheese cubes in his mouth.

"Don't be silly we are a team," I said to Colin.

"So why didn't you ask for another picture?" Molly asked.

"I didn't want to. With everything going on I'm happy not to be in the paper. It's hard enough seeing the violence and fear in my job without worrying that I might be next," I said. Officer Myers put a bowl of gravy on the table and took the seat next to me.

"Oh he is yummy," Molly pointed to the picture of Austin over Trevor's shoulder and made a sound. The type of sound you would make when eating a delicious dessert.

"You know I'm right here, right?" Trevor asked.

"Sorry, love." She kissed him lightly on the lips and sat next to him. "Does he work with you?"

"We have worked with him on a few cases," Colin said.

"I have a date with him tomorrow," I said.

"She almost had it tonight," Colin said.

"I wouldn't be mad if you did," Molly said. "I know it's been a while since you dated. You'll have to write down everything that happened on the date, so you can tell me when I get back."

"I won't leave anything out, unless it's embarrassing," I

said.

"I don't think you will have much to write down," Colin said.

"What?" Molly asked, while she took a piece of roast beef and passed it to Trevor.

"He's not a Survivor," Colin said splatting a spoonful of potatoes on his plate.

"So? You date girls that aren't Survivors," Molly said.

"Yeah, but my side effect doesn't affect my date in any way," Colin said.

"It does because she will not understand what it's like to be one of us," Molly said.

"I don't know why that matters. Does it mean someone with a disability can't fall in love with someone who is perfectly healthy, because they can't understand the hardship? Or someone who is an opera singer can't date anyone who can't carry a tune, because they don't understand what it's like to have that gift?" Officer Myers asked.

"True, besides, Claire has learned to control her ability with all of us," Molly said.

"Yeah but she can't control it all the time, even with us," Trevor said. He was thinking of the last time he'd tried to surprise Molly with a trip only to discover that she was already packed when he got here. How was I supposed to know it was a surprise?

"So what, I can never get married or even date because sometimes I slip and read other people's thoughts?" I asked.

"It's not what we mean," Trevor said. "It would be easier and less frightening to someone else who is a Survivor. You might even find someone who is hard for you to read their mind like Colin."

"Survivors treat me the same as non-Survivors," I swirled the wine in my glass. "I tell someone what I can do and they clench up and sing songs in their heads because they're scared I will find something embarrassing about them. Like some of you are doing now."

Molly cleared her throat after a moment of uncomfortable silence and asked Colin, "Is this detective a nice guy?"

"Yeah, I guess," Colin said.

"Then there isn't a problem." Molly nodded her head at me. "How am I going to get nieces if she never dates?"

We spent the rest of dinner talking about Trevor's and Molly's wedding. Molly enjoyed showing us sample invitations in a gazillion font variations. Trevor and Colin smiled and nodded along with as much enthusiasm as they could. At the end of dinner Molly said, "We have moved the wedding date from Christmas to two months from today."

"Is that safe?" Officer Myers asked. I had forgotten the detective was eating dinner with us. He had remained quiet throughout the discussion of the wedding, with the exception of a few head nods.

"It's going to have to be." Molly held Trevor's hand. "I'm pregnant."

Colin and I took turns hugging Molly and Trevor. I wasn't surprised when Officer Myers also congratulated the couple with a hug for Molly and a firm handshake for Trevor.

"How long have you known?" I asked.

"I just found out," Molly said.

"Are you excited about being Aunt Claire?" Molly asked. I could feel tears forming in my eyes.

"I'm going to be an aunt," I said my voice cracking. "I like the sound of that. Did you tell Mom?"

"No, we are waiting until she gets back from her trip," Molly said. Our mother is an anthropologist who has been on a dig in Mexico for the last few months. She wasn't due back for another three weeks.

"I guess this means you won't be going with Trevor," Colin said.

"What do you mean?" she asked.

"It's more risky now that you're pregnant. It doesn't take much to lose a baby," I said.

"Even stress is bad," Colin said.

"I'm not stressed by going. I will only be stressed if I have to be away from Trevor. Always wondering if he is hurt," Molly said.

"You're letting her go?" I looked accusingly at Officer Myers and Trevor.

"It's her choice," Officer Myers said.

"You think I can stop her?" Trevor asked with a laugh.

"This is big news. Something I have been wanting to tell you guys. Please, for tonight can we just be happy about the baby?" Molly asked.

"You're right this is your night," I said. Colin and I asked her endless questions about the pregnancy from vitamins to the due date. I forced myself to laugh and smile with everyone else. I was growing increasingly queasy. I couldn't push away the feeling of dread that was growing inside me.

CHAPTER FIFTEEN

The next morning, I woke up early and waited in the living room for Molly to come out of her room. I gave up, two hours later when I knew I was going to be late for work. I wrote a note on the fridge, "I hope you're still here when I get home so we can say good-bye. Love Claire."

Colin was sitting at his desk talking to a young woman with long black hair pulled back in a barrette. She turned around after I walked into the room, and saw she had soft almond-shaped eyes.

"Claire, I'd like you to meet someone," Colin said. "This is Zoe. She works down on the second floor in Minor Disputes."

"It's nice to meet you," I said.

"Likewise," Zoe said.

"What can we do for you?" I asked taking a seat at my desk.

"Mrs. Lewis told me that you might have time to help me with one of my cases," Zoe said.

"Gail knows that the detectives are taking the day off and we finished our last case. Kind-hearted as she is, she thought we might need something to occupy our time."

Zoe's thoughts became as clear and audible as a normal voice. *I can't believe I'm doing this. I really didn't want to be the first in my department that asked for help, but I'm afraid of what will happen if this doesn't get solved soon.*

"We'd be more than happy to help. It's hard to do this job on your own. I couldn't imagine doing it without a partner," I said. Colin sighed, pulling his eyes away from his computer screen, which by the sound of the mouse clicking and his idle glances he had to be checking on his Fantasy Baseball league.

"Thank you." Zoe nodded her head. "Would you like to ride with me? Or would you rather drive?"

"Drive where?" Colin asked.

"Gilroy," Zoe said.

Colin chose to drive us to Gilroy. No big surprise there. After we drove a few miles on the freeway Colin asked, "Why is your case all the way in Gilroy?"

"I was assigned to work the Gilroy area," she said.

"The whole city?" Colin looked at Zoe sitting in the seat next to him.

"I rotate days with another co-worker. Gilroy is coping well with the news. We haven't had many problems, other than a little bickering between neighbors."

"No murders? Or violence?" I asked. I was so focused on my own cases; I hadn't thought that the other cities might be handling this differently.

"No murders." After a few moments she added, "We had a bar fight a few days ago with a group of Survivors and a group of non-Survivors. Though after further investigation, I found the true cause of the fight was a girl who had just dumped one of the men who wasn't a Survivor to go out with one who was."

"Sounds calmer than San Jose – makes me want to move there," Colin said.

"It's a great town if you can handle the smell," Zoe said.

"What about the smell?" Colin asked.

"Don't tell him. He hasn't been through the city before," I whispered from behind the seat.

"Don't tell me what?" He asked. We both laughed. "Don't make me pull over and Google it."

"You'll know soon enough," I cackled, which made Zoe

giggle. Colin sighed. He was used to being ganged up on by girls.

Colin was focusing on his driving. I had the urge to tease him, but tried to suppress it. Colin caught me smiling in the rearview mirror, his large bushy eyebrows dancing. "What?"

"I was just thinking it must be hard to drive the speed limit on the freeway with only three other cars on the road. I think that was a little old lady who just passed us."

Zoe observed Colin's face and said, "I guess I should tell you about my case."

"That would be nice," Colin said.

"There's a farmer by the name of John. He took over running his dad's farm this year after his father suffered a severe back injury in a car accident. This year only John's farm had a good lettuce crop. The other farmers are blaming John for their misfortune."

"Do you think he is doing it on purpose?" I asked.

"I think he has a side effect that affects crops, I'm just not sure how. He seems pretty clueless about it as well," she said.

The strong smell of garlic wafted through the car. The smell was so strong I didn't need to see any signs or landmarks to know we had reached Gilroy.

"What is that?" Colin asked.

"Garlic. There's lots of farms growing it here," I said.

"Turn down the next road, we're meeting John at his place, first, and then we'll meet with the other farmers once we know something," Zoe said.

Colin pulled into the driveway and stopped at the house. When we got out of the car, Colin started choking. "That can't be garlic."

"What else could it be?" I asked.

"I might believe they are growing thousands of dirty gym socks from high school boys," Colin said. Thanks to his side effect, Colin has a very strong sense of smell; I couldn't imagine how he copes around potent smells.

A young man, in jeans and a cowboy hat, ambled up to our car. When he came closer, I could see he had dark brown eyes and a broad face filled with freckles. He smiled and said, "Thanks for coming, Zoe."

"I'm happy to come," Zoe said. She flushed as John gave her another smile. "I brought some help. This is Claire and Colin; they work with me back at my office in San Jose."

"Nice to meet you both." He shook our hands. I could feel deep cuts and calluses on his palm.

"So how do we do this?" John looked at Colin.

"Could you give us a tour of your farm before we talk to the other farmers?" Colin asked. "We need to get a sense of how they are different."

"Sure, but I don't know how much help it will be." John shrugged. "I have no idea why our lettuce is doing so much better than our neighbors. We use all the same stuff, even shop at the same suppliers."

As he spoke, he started leading us past the house toward the lettuce fields. Colin kept him talking by asking question about the weather this spring and summer, water allotments and other crops that were grown on the fields we would be looking at. He knew that I needed to listen to John's thoughts and I couldn't talk and listen at the same time. Zoe didn't add much to the conversation since she had already asked these questions, according to her thoughts.

Before we got to the field we passed by a rose garden and the thought of water popped into John's head. He stopped and turned on the sprinkler. It was a little strange because he wasn't even looking at the roses as we passed them.

When we got to the lettuce field I started to wish I had a fork and some salad dressing on me. It was the best lettuce I had ever seen. The heads were large and looked crisp. There wasn't a wilted leaf in the entire field. John suddenly started thinking about giant weeds and veered three rows over. There he bent down to pull out a dandelion that had gotten in with the lettuce. It wasn't very tall so where did the giant image come from?

We headed back to the house through an immature carrot field. The guys had switched to talking baseball which was much easier for me to tune out than the more fascinating agricultural topics. Halfway down the field, John was hit with a wave of fear. John turned right and said, "Darn gophers! I'll need to come back and put some traps out." I looked where he had turned and there was a gopher mound I hadn't noticed before.

"John, could we please stop for a minute? I'd like to try an experiment."

"Sure, what do you want to do?" John asked.

"I'd like you to go to the fence and close your eyes," I said.

After he reached the fence, I went toward a row of carrots and started to pull them up. John whirled around and said, "What are you doing?"

"A more interesting question would be 'how did you know I was doing something damaging to the carrots?'" I asked. "I know you felt a wave of anguish before you turned around."

"Huh? I just felt uncomfortable," John said.

"I think you have a very close connection to plants," I said. "You knew the roses needed water before you looked at them. And that dandelion you pulled wasn't as big as it seemed in your mind so I'm guessing that's how the lettuce saw it."

"That's just crazy," John chuckled. "Plants don't talk"

"They may not talk to most people but they are definitely communicating with you," I said.

"Claire's talent is to know things about people that they may not even know themselves, so I'd recommend believing her," Colin said. "I have a talent similar to yours with dogs and their kin. Dogs don't exactly talk either but I can sense what they are feeling and get images from them."

"I guess that explains what my dad was trying to tell me. I never thought when he said I was special, he meant this,"

John said.

"John, can we tell the other farmers about this?" Zoe asked. John was still gawking at his field of lettuce. After a moment Zoe touched his arm gently. "Do you want them to know? Are you willing to share your ability to help them?"

"You haven't steered me wrong yet." John turned around and looked down at Zoe. "I'll do anything to fix this. They all think I've cursed their lands so it can't be worse to tell them the truth."

"Ok, let's call a meeting at the grange hall in an hour," Zoe said pulling out her cell phone.

We went into the house and visited with John's dad while John and Zoe called the farmers and arranged the meeting. Mr. Miller gave us lemonade made from lemons grown on the farm and it was better than any lemonade I've ever had.

About half the farmers were there when we arrived and the mood was a little tense while we waited for the others. Zoe pointed out Luke the ringleader, among the farmers. He was taller than the rest of the farmers and chewed on a toothpick as he talked to each farmer in the group. Luke was the first to speak. "Are you going to make that boy take the curse off our farms?" A mummer of agreement swept through the crowd.

"We've done some research and we believe that it's a blessing on the Millers' farm rather than a curse on all of your farms," Colin said. "You're already aware that John is a Survivor?"

After some murmuring among them, the farmers nodded in agreement.

"The plague has left John with a gift. Plants communicate their needs to him and because he is a farm boy, he responds," Zoe said.

"I remember the first year after John recovered from the, plague. He won first prize in the 4H competition at the county fair for his tomatoes," said one of the men in the back of the group.

"And every year after that," said another man.

Still belligerent, Luke said, "How does that help us? He might have a better lettuce crop this year but what about the strawberries? Most of us lost our strawberries this year to a late frost and the Millers' farm didn't because John planted later than we did. I might be able to accept that already growing plants communicate with him but not seeds."

"John, how did you know to plant later?" I asked.

"Hmmm, well, I do seem to anticipate extreme weather, frost, heat waves, storms, but my grandpa had a toe that bothered him just before it rained so I didn't think anything of it," he said.

"You could have told us," Luke said.

"I'm at least two decades younger than you all and you still call me 'boy'. Would you have believed me if I had said anything?" John asked.

There was grumbling but I could tell that they all recognized the truth of what John said.

Zoe asked, "Where do we go from here? Are you now willing to listen to John about the weather and your crops?"

"Hell, yes," Luke said. "I'm even willing to pay him for his time if he'll come look over my farm every couple of weeks and let me know what needs to be done."

Colin looked at me and I nodded. The farmers' thoughts indicated hope rather than anger now and it was safe for us to leave them to work out the details themselves.

As we left I gave my card to John and told him that our office was developing some training programs to help Survivors make the most of their gifts and to feel free to come by anytime.

Gail followed me into our office with a large stack of papers. She placed the towering stack on Colin's desk. "What's this?" Colin asked.

"I'm not surprised you don't recognize it. It's your paper work due by the end of the day," Gail said.

"The end of the day?" Colin rifled through some of the

papers, "It's going to take hours to write every detail of what I did."

"If you did it every day like you're supposed to this wouldn't be a problem." Gail looked down at him. "Do you need another lecture on how to do the paperwork?"

"No." He sighed.

"Good. If you have any questions ask Claire. She hands her paperwork in every day."

"I will," Colin glared at me, while I sat at my desk and smiled.

After Gail left the office, he said, "I've got a date tonight. I don't suppose you'd be willing to help me with some of this?"

"Oh, the way you helped me the other day? I think your exact words were 'How can I help you when I didn't experience it?' Besides, I have a date tonight," I said with a smile.

CHAPTER SIXTEEN

By the time I got home from work that evening, Molly and Trevor had already left. Molly left a note on the fridge, "I went with Trevor. Don't worry. Love Molly."

I didn't have time to dwell on her being gone, because I was running late for my date. I was reminded about how long it had been since I had last dated by the lack of appropriate dating outfits in my closet. My bedroom quickly became reminiscent of a five-year-old's room, with clothes spread like heaps of snow. I decided on wearing a dark green summer dress with black heels.

I had just finished applying my mascara when the doorbell rang.

Austin eyed me up and down, with a slight smile. He didn't smile often so I took it as a compliment. He was wearing a button up white shirt and a red and black tie, black slacks and black shoes and holding a small bouquet of pink lilies.

"These are for you." He handed me the flowers.

"Thank you," I smiled and put them in a crystal vase in the kitchen.

We walked down to his car, a silver Mustang. He opened the door and I slid into the seat. After a few minutes I asked, "So where are we going?"

"You'll see," he said in a serious voice that told me that was the only answer I was getting.

We went up through the mountains towards the ocean. Driving through the mountains reminded me of lands designed for fantasy stories. A gentle mist hung through the swaying pine trees that gave the illusion that everything was alive with movement. When we finally came to a stop he turned off the keys and said, "We're here."

Austin came around and opened my door. I got out and looked around. We were at a parking lot overlooking the beach. The only building in sight looked like an old blue Victorian home that must have been converted into a restaurant. As we got closer, I could see a sign on the lawn that read "Pearls by the Sea". The scene would have been perfect if there wasn't a line of picketers in front of the restaurant.

"Nice view, except for the protestors," I said.

"Funny, Aunt Pearl didn't say anything about this when I made the reservation," Austin said.

"Aunt Pearl?" I asked.

"Yes, my Aunt Pearl owns this place. Look, this isn't what I expected this to be like. Do you still want to have dinner here or shall we go someplace else?" Austin asked.

"There seem to be protesters wherever we go these days, so we might as well eat here," I said with a smile.

We approached the picket line together. One of the protestors stopped and stepped out of line to talk to us. He wore a police uniform and despite his grey hair he looked young. He said, "You guys look like a nice couple. I wouldn't want to see you get hurt."

"Are you threatening us?" Austin asked.

"Not at all. It's the man inside you should be worried about. The cook is a Survivor. We've been trying to get rid of him for days, but the owner won't fire him. She is even letting him live there," the police officer said.

"We'll take our chances. Thanks for the warning." Austin took my hand and we walked through the picket line to the door of the restaurant. He held the door for me as we entered. The hallway had been turned into the hostess stand. The living room had eight tables all dressed in matching white tablecloths. There was only one table in use by an elderly couple.

A woman in her early twenties with a cute pixie cut that well suited her triangular face and plump lips came to the stand and said, "Hey, Austin."

"Hi, Amber. What's with the protestors? How long have they been there?"

"A few days and it has been getting more tense as time goes on." She nodded toward a side window that had been broken and boarded over.

"Have you called the police?" Austin asked. "Protesting is one thing but vandalism is a crime."

"The Chief of Police is one of the protestors so I don't think it would do us much good to call them. And you know your aunt, she isn't going to back down," Amber said with a sigh.

"What do they want?" Austin asked. "The guy out there mentioned your cook."

"Our cook, Craig, was the first person in our town to survive the plague, so those yahoos think he has some dangerous side effect. They have overlooked the simple fact that he was in his thirties when he got the plague and all the research says that majority of the people who have side effects caught the disease before or during puberty."

She suddenly noticed me and grinned. "I'm glad to see you brought a girl for once." Amber looked at every inch of me and then nodded in approval. "Are you a friend that's a girl or a girl friend?"

I honestly didn't know what I was or wanted to be. I was about to speak but an older woman with white hair done up in braids came from behind Amber and said, "Give the boy a chance. You'll scare her away. I caught her eyeing the exits when you asked that question." She winked at me and I laughed. She turned to Austin and threw her arms up, "Aren't you going to introduce us?"

"Yes, ma'am, this is Claire" Austin nodded his head

toward me, "She was that girl I told you about. The one I worked with before I moved to Homicide."

"Yes, I remember, I'm not senile. You called in your reservation just yesterday." She sounded serious but I could tell she was teasing him by the smile on her face.

"Well, it's nice to meet you, Claire," the old woman hugged me and I couldn't decide if I was more surprised by the gesture or the fact it didn't seem odd. "I'm Aunt Pearl and this is my daughter Amber."

"It's nice to meet both of you," I said.

"All right you show them up to their table, and no more teasing. Not unless she makes it past the third date," Aunt Pearl said.

"Follow me." Amber grinned wickedly. Austin bent down and wrapped the old woman in his arms and said, "Thank you, but we need to talk about those protestors before we leave."

I noticed Amber eyeing me oddly, as we walked up the stairs. I read her thoughts and found out that she was debating if it was appropriate to ask if I was a Survivor, too, since Austin had mentioned last week that he had a friend who was a Survivor. It was a small town and she was feeling lonely, not having met very many other Survivors her age.

The room had many tables, but only one of them was set. It sat by the window overlooking the ocean. Amber lit the white candle in the middle of our table.

She was about to leave when I asked, "Aren't there menus?"

"No, but don't worry, Craig always knows what to make," Amber said.

"Come here often?" I asked after Amber left.

"Yeah. My aunt started this place a few years ago. I get to visit my aunt and cousin and get a good meal as a bonus."

The lights dimmed and Austin sighed and I laughed. "I know they mean well."

A few minutes later, Amber came back with a bottle of wine and filled our glasses.

"Could I ask you a question?" Austin asked.

"You already did." He looked at me with a stiff face. "Go ahead."

"Do you remember the first time we met two year ago on the beauty queen case?" Austin asked.

"Yes." It was hard to forget that case. It took parent involvement in afterschool activities to a whole new level. One of the mother's was causing horrific accidents that left many of her daughter's competition in the hospital.

"You had told me that you were able to point out the killer because you saw her do it in a dream. You said you were psychic."

"Is there a question coming?" I asked.

"Well I guess I didn't believe you back then. I thought you were good at figuring things out but I always thought it was because you were overly observant. With the news of the Survivors, I'm wondering is it true? Are you a psychic?" Austin asked.

I buttered a piece of bread and took a bite so I could think. I had only told one person that I have dated that wasn't a fellow Survivor about my special abilities. It was my high school boyfriend, and let me tell you nothing kills the mood like being crowned prom queen while your boyfriend grabs the microphone to announce to your whole school that you're nuts.

"You don't have to tell me," he said.

This wasn't high school anymore. I had to try to open up to someone or I would never get close to anyone. I took a deep breath. "You can't tell other people what I can do. Not even your family or your partner." He nodded as I spoke. "I can do a few things. I can read other people's thoughts."

"A telepath." He nodded to indicate to go on.

"I can also feel other people's emotions. I hesitated a moment and decided not to tell him about the full extent my other abilities. Two were enough for now.

"Really?" I could see his eyes moving as he is processed

what to say next. "Is that how you knew that Mike and Nadine Foster killed Mrs. Cooper?"

"Well I know that Nadine was involved in the murder."

"I hear a but coming," Austin said.

"Here's the thing. Nadine's thoughts, memories and emotions all point to her being involved. Mike on the other hand, has nothing that points to him doing it. Except that through Nadine's memory I could see him do it."

Austin drank some of his wine and then said, "Did you ever think that he could be delusional?"

"I don't follow," I said.

"Well if Mike has some psychiatric disorder he might not remember anything accurately. Maybe he had a psychotic episode or was hallucinating at the time of the murder. Or maybe he has memory loss."

"I don't know, I guess it could happen. I have had people lie in their thoughts before." Austin was staring at me. I read his thoughts and repeated them out loud. "You doubt I can do it? You want to see proof."

"A five-year-old could pick up on that. I'm a cop, of course, I want solid proof. Logically, it would be easy to make the connection that Mike and Nadine could have done the crime with just a little digging."

"Ok think of your most prized possession," I said and his thoughts scanned the various objects he had stored in his home.

"Your dad's police shield given to you at his funeral." I repeated his thoughts.

Austin looked pale. "So you know my other thoughts?"

"I try not to listen, but sometimes it's too hard. It's like someone screaming in your ear," I said.

"Anything embarrassing?" He cleared his throat. "From me, I mean."

"No different from any other man I have been around. Though the pirate outfits are interesting."

"I love pirate movies." He coughed and looked away.

"It's ok if you can't handle this," I said.

"Let's get one thing straight. I can handle anything." Austin put down his wine glass and took my hand. "It will take time to get used to it. But I like you. All of you."

My first date jitters started to melt away but before we could continue exchanging romantic pleasantries, Amber returned with our food. We spent the next few minutes giving our undivided attention to the fabulous chicken parmesan that she brought us.

Amber reappeared when we finished to clear away our plates and bring us some luscious looking chocolate cake, one piece with two forks.

As I picked up my fork, I asked Austin, "Are your cousin and aunt trying to tell me something by bring one dessert with two forks?"

Austin looked sheepish. "They really do mean well. It's been a long time since I've been out and I very rarely bring a girl here."

"I feel honored. I haven't been out in a long time either," I said.

After the cake, we headed downstairs to say good-bye to Amber and Aunt Pearl. We both wanted to know more about the protestors outside. Most of the protestors had gone home when the sun went down.

"So, Aunt Pearl, what do you plan to do about the protestors?" Austin asked.

"I'm not giving them Craig nor am I going to shut down. They'll get tired of it and go home eventually," Aunt Pearl said.

"What are you planning on doing if they don't go away?" Austin asked.

"I have a gun in the back if need be, and yes, it's registered, Detective Hughes."

Austin opened his mouth to respond and I laid a hand on his arm to stop him. "Before it gets to that point, please give us a call." I handed Aunt Pearl one of my business cards. "If you need it there is a sanctuary in the same building as our office."

When we arrived back at my apartment, I turned around to thank him, but instead his lips met mine. I felt the rush of desire and I wasn't sure if it was mine or Austin's or both. We stayed in that kiss a few moments. When he pulled away I was going to invite him in for coffee, but before I could, a high-pitched buzzing sound came from Austin pocket. "I'm sorry. It's work. I will only be a minute."

I opened the door, I went to the kitchen to start a pot of coffee, and Austin took his phone call in the living room. I watched him walk back and forth next to the window. The sounds of the coffee maker and his low voice made it impossible to listen to his phone call.

When he came into the kitchen, he said, "That was Detective Moseley. He was called in. He's at Trevor's safe house. There was an attack."

"But he's a homicide detective."

"All I know is that both Trevor and Molly are being rushed to the county hospital."

"I need to call my mom." I picked up my cell phone from out of my purse. My hands shook so much that I dropped it.

Austin picked up the phone and placed it in my hand. "If you need me to stay. I can ask someone else to take over for me at the crime scene."

"No, it's ok. I can handle this. I'd rather you handle the murder. Besides, they are likely to let only family in," I said. He bent down and kissed me on the cheek, I felt tingly all over in spite of my worry.

"I understand. If you need anything. Call me anytime." He reached over and unplugged the coffee maker as he left the kitchen.

I called my mother after Austin left, to tell her what had happened. I told her that Molly was pregnant. My mother was taking the next flight out. I was relieved. I couldn't handle taking care of Molly alone. On the way to my car, I called Sean and Colin. Sean said he'd meet me at the hospital but I wasn't able to reach Colin.

I could hear Sean yelling as soon as the glass doors opened into the emergency room. An older doctor with white hair was attempting to calm him down.

"It's been almost half an hour, and they can't tell me what's wrong with her," Sean said as I walked up to him. "You'd think a doctor wouldn't be so incompetent!"

"I'm sure they are doing their best," I said. "How is my sister doing?"

"We don't know yet. The pregnancy and the amount of injuries she suffered are causing some complications," the doctor said turning away from Sean to talk to me. "She suffered a knife wound in the abdomen near her liver and a head injury. We sent her for an ultrasound and we're waiting on the surgeon now. When we know anything we will tell you. For now I need to go back to seeing patients."

"Thank you for taking the time to tell us," I said as the doctor walked away.

"What about Trevor?" I asked

"He didn't make it," he said. I felt my heart stop. My whole body shook. My eyes stung from holding back tears. I took a deep breath. I couldn't fall apart right now. "Where's Colin?"

"He didn't answer his phone but I know he's on a date so he may be ignoring it. He probably won't check his phone until after the date is over."

Colin had made it to the hospital a few minutes later. I walked up to him. I couldn't think of anything to say. I just fell into his chest. He draped his arms around me and I cried.

We spent the next few hours in the hospital lobby on a sofa that felt like sandpaper and had more wood than stuffing in its cushions. We spent our time watching three fish that swam around in a dirty fish tank. Every half and hour or so a nurse would come over and update us.

It was nearly two in the morning when Molly finally got

out of surgery. She had a minor concussion and a punctured liver. The surgeon managed to fix her liver without harming the baby. He said we could go see her but she wouldn't be very lucid due to the pain medication which he assured us would not harm the baby.

Colin rubbed a hand down my arm as we walked towards her room.

"How do we tell her?" I asked.

"She might already know, Just be there. It's all you can do," Sean said. They waited outside her room; they knew she would not want them to see her in a flimsy hospital gown.

"Hey," Molly took a deep breath in and closed her eyes.

"How are you?" I held her right hand and I could feel her body jerk. "Are you in any pain?"

"Not much, they gave me the good stuff." She pointed to her IV. "Jealous?"

"It must be good if you're up to teasing me." I brushed back the strands of brown hair that shielded her eyes.

"I'm ok, Trevor has been with me this whole time."

"Sweetie, Trevor died before coming to the hospital."

"Silly, Trevor is standing by the window. He hasn't left me this whole time." I knew what was happening. I think she knew, too.

"There is no one there." I looked at the window. "Ask him if he died."

"Honey tell her you're alive." Her eyes traveled the room. "He said he is not going to leave me. It's going to be ok he said." I didn't know what to say, I didn't know if what she was saying was real or the medication talking.

"Why don't you get some sleep? We can talk about it in the morning." I held her hand as she drifted off to sleep.

CHAPTER SEVENTEEN

I woke up to the faint sound of my cell phone ringing from my purse that was sitting on the counter in the kitchen. I recognized the ringtone as the song from *The Twilight Zone*, which is the ringtone I reserved for work numbers. I wanted to get up to answer the phone but Rosie was lounging on my stomach like a hammock, yipping in her sleep. This act would be adorable, if it wasn't for the fact that she was an 80-pound German shepherded mix with the delusions of being a small lap dog.

After the fifth time the phone rang I regretfully tore myself out of my warm bed into the cold morning air. I dragged myself down the hall, my eyes still blurry. I tripped and fell face first onto the living room floor. I stood up and saw a smile pile of suitcases. I knew the suitcases belonged to my mother, because of the neon yellow ribbons that were tied on each handle. The phone was still ringing, so I walked to the kitchen counter and picked it up. I recognized the caller ID.

"Hello, Austin," I said.

"Good morning, Claire," Austin said.

"It's not morning until I have my coffee," I said with a sigh as I saw the clock read, six am. I had only been asleep for two hours.

"I'm sorry to call you so early," Austin said. "When you work crazy hours it's hard to remember that other people sleep in on the weekends."

"I don't mind," I said. "I'd have had to get up soon anyway. Visiting hours start soon at the hospital. What can I do for you?"

"I'm lead detective on the murder of Trevor and the attempted murder of your sister. I was hoping you and Colin might have time today to help with the investigation," Austin said.

"Is this to help solve the crime or simply to help the police image after they neglected to keep two Survivors safe while in police protection." I could hear him suck in his breath as I talked.

"I can see how you might think that. To be honest with you it's a bit of both," he said.

"At least you're honest. I'm going to the hospital to sit with Molly until visiting hours are over. If you need to talk to me you can find me there."

"I'm sorry about your sister." Austin voice softened, "How is she doing?"

"The doctor says she will make a full recovery."

"That's good to hear. I hope she gets better. I will need to talk to her about the attack. When would be a good time?"

"Let me assess the situation at the hospital and call you back."

"OK, I'll wait until I hear from you."

When I reached Molly's hospital room, my mom was in a green chair by her bed. Other than sharing the same green eyes, we looked nothing alike. In fact she looks more like Molly's mother than my own. She looked up at me when I entered the room and I could tell she had been crying. I gave her a hug before taking the other chair next to her.

"How is she doing?" I asked.

"You know Molly, she never complains but I can tell that she's hurting," Mom said. "The doctor came by and is pleased with her progress. They're limiting her pain medication so that she can get off it more quickly because of the baby."

"Can you believe you're going to be a grandmother?" I asked.

"This isn't how I wanted to find out. We were so far away from civilization that I didn't even know that the reaction to Trevor's research had been so negative and violent. Why didn't you tell me?"

I shrugged. "Away on the dig there really wasn't anything you could do and I didn't want to worry you."

"I'm your mother. It's my job to worry about you two. If I'd known, I would have come back immediately. No dig is worth not being near enough to help you when you need it."

"I'll keep that in mind next time," I said.

Molly started to stir so we lapsed into silence. We spent most of the morning reading. We watched silently as the nurses came in and out to check on Molly who was sleeping. I was about three-fourths of the way done with a classic Anne Perry mystery that I'd found in the hospital library, when I looked over the top of my book and found that Molly was sitting in her bed talking to herself.

"Molly?" I asked. "Are you ok? Do you need something?"

"Oh, no I'm sorry to interrupt your reading. I was just talking to Trevor," Molly said.

I put my book down and walked over to her. "Molly, you do know that he died yesterday."

"I do." Her eyes fluttered to stay awake. "But only his body died, his ghost stayed with me."

"How long will Trevor stay with you?" Mom asked.

"I don't know." Her eyes became distant and then said, "He said he tried to leave but can't. Oh, isn't it just wonderful?"

My mother stood on the other side of her and ran her fingers through Molly's hair. We looked at each other not knowing what to say. Spending the rest of your life with your true love, and not being able to touch him, marry him or raise kids with him. I couldn't imagine it. Not to mention, if she ever found someone else it would be very cruel to Trevor.

"I hope it's wonderful for both of you," my mother said and I agreed.

"Are you up for talking about what happened last night?" I asked.

"Well I suppose so. It's not like I'm going anywhere anytime soon."

"Let me give Austin a call so you don't have to go through this twice."

When Austin got there, he agreed that I should ask the questions. "Do you or Trevor remember anything about the night you were attacked?" I asked.

"Trevor?" Austin asked.

"Just go with it. I'll explain later," I said.

After a few moments of listening to a one sided conversation Molly was having with Trevor, she said, "Trevor doesn't remember much. He was watching TV and he thought he heard footsteps behind him. Before he could turn around someone put a hand over his mouth and he felt a sharp pain in his stomach. Not long after everything went dark."

"I'm so sorry," I said to the air around me hoping I was saying it to Trevor. Her eyes filled with tears.

"Do you remember anything?" I asked Molly.

"I remember I was taking a shower and I heard a large thump like a person tripped and fell. So I got my towel and peeked outside. I saw Officer Olsson. The odd thing was he looked surprised to see me. He grabbed my mouth and slammed me down on to the floor. Before I blacked out he said "You weren't on the list. You aren't supposed to be here."

"Were you not supposed to be there?" I asked.

"Yes, I was supposed to be there." She nodded. "I

don't know what he meant because he saw me earlier that evening."

"Do you know what list he was talking about?" I asked.

"No," she said.

I was about to ask her if Trevor knew what the list was, but just before I did her eyes closed and she drifted off to sleep. Molly didn't wake up again during visiting hours except for brief periods of pain.

I went to meet Colin and the detectives at the office as soon as visiting hours were over. The office was practically deserted that evening. Not many lights were on, and the only noise I heard was the sounds of the cleaning staff vacuuming the hallway to the office.

I found Colin and Austin in our office. "I'm sorry to keep you waiting," I said sitting in my chair. "Where's Detective Moseley?"

"He said he had a family matter to deal with and couldn't stay," Austin said.

"What have you found out so far?" I asked.

"The good news is that during the time of the attack only two officers had access to the victims. Which means the only logical explanation is that one or both of the men did the crime," Austin said.

"What's the bad news?" I asked.

"The bad news is that we may have a much bigger problem," Austin said.

"What could possibly be bigger than Trevor's murder and my sister's attack?" I snapped.

"I'm sorry you're right," Austin said gently. "I will rephrase. Not bigger just another problem. The murder resembles the Cooper murder a little too closely."

"Aren't the killers in jail?" Colin asked interrupting Austin.

"Yes," Austin said. "I'm not suggesting it's the same killer. Let me just explain. Trevor was killed in a similar way. Stabbing to the chest and he was smothered no doubt to keep him from alarming the neighbors since he was in a thinly walled hotel. Trevor had the first half of the word traitor carved in his chest, but it looks like Molly interrupted him. Molly's attack seems unplanned because the attacker only stabbed her once and didn't hit the vital organs like he did with Mrs. Cooper and Trevor and there was no attempt to carve anything on her chest."

Austin took out a plastic bag containing a piece of paper and showed it to me. It was the same poster found at Mrs. Cooper's crime scene with the pictures of the top twenty Survivors. This time two pictures were crossed out in blood, Mrs. Cooper and Trevor. It dawned on me that this was the list the killer told Molly she wasn't on; she was never part of the killer's plan.

"You think it might be the, Brotherhood of Humanity, group that is behind the murders?" I asked.

"I do." Austin nodded. "I think they're planning on killing everyone on the list. We're in the process of identifying everyone on the list so we can warn them. If you know anyone on the list you should warn them to be extra careful."

"Why because you think all Survivors know each other?" Colin asked.

"I didn't mean it that way and you know it." Austin pointed a finger at Colin.

I looked down and studied the faces on the poster. Some of the faces had changed from the first time I saw the poster. I saw a few people I recognized as working with Trevor, but one picture stood out. "Alice is on the list." I pointed to an older picture of Alice on the bottom row. Austin looked blankly at me so I added, "She's my friend. We went to school together."

"Why would she be on the list?" Austin asked.

"The news covered her bakery," I said. Austin didn't understand but Colin did.

"We will help in any way we can. What do you need us to do?" Colin asked.

"I need to know which one did the crime. There were

no fingerprints on the murder weapon and there is no other physical evidence to point to who did it since any fingerprints or hair can be explained by the officers staying in the hotel room. The only thing we have to go on is the statements of the officers and Molly. Officer Myers claims Officer Olsson committed the crime while he was on duty. Officer Olsson claims that he has no memory of doing the crime."

"If the crime happened at night, wouldn't Officer Olsson have been on duty?" I asked. I had become all too aware of his work schedule, when he was at my apartment at night.

"No, they switched shifts with the help of another officer when they moved to the hotel," Austin said.

"Will you interview them?" Austin asked. "Someone is lying, and I don't want to ruin the wrong cop's life. I was hoping you could verify their stories."

"Do you know what you're asking me to do?" I started to feel queasy at the thought of having to see any part of the attack. It was hard enough to see death in a stranger's memories. It was a whole different story when it's my sister.

"I hate that I have to ask. If you can't handle it I will try to find another way to figure this out," Austin said.

"No, Molly deserves answers," I said. "It will have to wait until morning. I can barely keep my own thoughts straight let alone someone else's."

The next morning, Colin drove me to the police station to interview the police officers. It was the same small room we had used to interview Mike. The only difference was that Colin went in with me instead of Austin.

Officer Myers was already waiting in the interview room. He had dark circles under his eyes and his head leaned down like a wilted flower.

"Good morning, Officer Myers," I said. He looked up at me with his pale dull eyes. "I'm just going to ask you a few questions about last night. Would that be all right with you?"

"Sure. I'd be happy to help." Officer Myers head leaned down.

"Can you give me your wrist?" I asked.

"Why?" Office Myers asked.

"To check for your pulse as you answer questions," Colin said quickly. It was easier to explain than the truth.

"All right." He raised an eyebrow and hesitantly gave me his right wrist.

"I want you to close your eyes and remember what happened yesterday from the moment you arrived in as much detail as you can. Try to say it and visualize it," I said.

I could see the room fade as another room emerged around me. It was one big room with lavender wallpaper, and country paintings of pigs and farms. I could see by the window that it was already dark.

"Sorry I'm late. Traffic was horrid," Officer Myers said to Officer Olsson sitting on a small purple sofa with his feet on the small glass table.

"No big deal. You're only keeping me from watching the same TV show at home," Officer Olsson said with a chuckle as he tore his head away from the small flat screen TV to gaze towards Officer Myers.

"What are you watching?" Officer Myers asked.

"I was watching a movie but it turned to a breaking news story," Officer Olsson said.

"Wait let me guess." I could see a large hand cover my view. "I bet it's a story on the Survivors."

"Yeah," He chuckled again and his stomach rumbled. "Another murder."

"I'm so glad we got this job. I'd hate to be out there," Office Myers said.

"It's a pretty easy job." He stretched and walked to the door. "Just babysitting them."

"See ya tomorrow, Derek," Officer Myers said.

"See, ya," Officer Olsson said.

Officer Myers walked towards the closed door at the end of the hall, and knocked. "This is Officer Myers, just letting you know I'm here."

"Thanks," a deep voice said over the muffled sounds of the TV and running water. He sat on the sofa, and changed the channel on the TV. After watching for a few minutes I realized it must be a reality show centered on the fashion world.

A few minutes later, a loud knock came at the door. Officer Myers jumped and turned the channel to a baseball game before going to the door. He looked through the hole on the door and saw it was Officer Olsson. "Geeze you scared me," he said opening the door.

"Sorry about that," Officer Olsson said.

"Why didn't you use the key?" He asked.

"Left it in the car," Officer Olsson chuckled and shook his head. "After a twelve-hour shift, the walk back to the car is too hard."

"We've all been there," Officer Myers said. "Why are you back?"

"Forgot something in the other room," he said as he walked towards the two closed rooms.

Officer Myers went back to the sofa and watched the baseball game. He glanced up when Officer Olsson turned the knob on the front door.

"Get what you needed?" Officer Myers asked.

"Yeah, I did." Officer Olsson smirked. He turned his reality show back on when the door shut.

He went to go get snacks from the mini bar when he heard soft moaning coming from the bedroom. He knocked on their door. "Is everything ok?" When no one answered he opened the door. I could see half of Trevor's long body lying on the floor the other half was covered by the bed.

I immediately let go of his wrist. "Stop thinking about it. Please stop." Colin pulled my shaking body into his chest. I couldn't make it stop.

Once, Officer Myers was out of the room I said, "He's telling the truth. He didn't have anything to do with the killing. He saved Molly's life by checking on them."

"Do you think you have time to evaluate Officer Olsson?" Austin asked.

"Why would she do that? It's obvious who did it," Colin said as he wrapped his hand on my shaking arm. "Don't you see what this does to her?"

"I'm sorry. I know I don't have any right to ask you to do this. I know the cop. Sure he's a bigot and an ass. But he doesn't seem like the type of person who could do this."

"Neither did Bundy," I said.

"True, but it's the only way to know for sure. If it's not too hard on you," Austin said.

"I'll try," I said.

Austin escorted Officer Olsson into the chair across from me. I stared at him. I have never hated anyone in my life. I didn't believe in hate but if I did I would hate him.

"I want you to remember as vividly as you can what happened after Officer Myers came to take your shift," I said placing my hand over his wrist.

Officer Olsson had the same memory as Officer Myers up until he left the hotel. I could see him walk out of the hotel room, and down a long hallway and rode the elevator. Officer Olsson walked across the deserted parking lot, humming a tune and swinging his keys. He stared at the broken light above his car. He shook his head as he opened the car door. When Officer Olsson sat down in the driver seat and shut the door, everything went black. Blurry images formed; I was staring at a clock. "Wow, I've got to stop pulling twelve-hour shifts," He laughed and started his car.

When the office slowly came back into focus, I could see that Colin was staring at Officer Olsson with a frown. The officer from outside came in and escorted him out.

When Austin rejoined us, I told them what I saw. "Something seems wrong about this," Colin said after a few moments of silence.

"I feel it too. But what?" I asked.

"We've got a witness. The desk clerk saw him going in and out of the hotel at the time of the murder. There are only two people other than the victims that could be in the hotel suite based on the key card data," Austin said.

I shrugged my shoulders at the detective's response. "What will happen to him?"

"He will mostly likely plead for an insanity defense," Austin said. "I don't think he will win even with the memory loss. There is just too much against him."

"I think it's time we start looking into the Brotherhood of Humanity. We need to find out what they're planning to do before someone else dies."

THE PUZZLE KEEPER

CHAPTER EIGHTEEN

Trevor's memorial service was held as soon as Molly was released from the hospital a few days later. It was a private service, only close friends and family, to avoid unwanted attention from the Brotherhood of Humanity. Even so, it was an awkward service with Molly making it clear that Trevor was in the room with us. Nothing stifles a memorial service like having the dead attend.

There was a larger private wake held at the pub the day after the service. Trevor's presence didn't spoil the festivities then because enough people were unaware that he was there. However, the Brotherhood of Humanity group must have found out about it because they stood in front of the bar protesting the party when I got there. I was surprised to find the bar full of people. I recognized many of the faces from the night we celebrated Trevor's research. It was hard to believe so much had happened since that night.

I spotted my mom and Molly talking to Sean next to the fireplace in the main dining area. They stopped talking when I walked up to them. I greeted everyone with a hug.

"Trevor says it would be too hard to see it with the grey stones of the fireplace," Molly said.

"But it's the best place to see it," Sean said.

"What's going on?" I asked my mom, tuning out their conversation.

"Sean is going to hang a picture of Trevor in the pub."

She pointed to a large framed picture of Trevor. "Trevor's being picky about the location. We've tried five places so far."

Sean sighed, "All right, show me where he wants the picture hung."

"Maybe over the bar?" Molly nodded as she looked at the bar. "Though he wants to see how it looks first."

He picked up the picture frame and they walked to the bar. "If he doesn't pick soon it's goin' in the men's room."

"Coming?" Mom asked.

"No, you go ahead." I saw Alice arranging baked goods on the long buffet table at the side of the bar. "I need to talk to someone." Mom nodded her head and walked towards the bar.

"Can I talk to you?" I asked as Alice was arranging a large basket of cookies on the table.

"Sure thing," she said.

"Have you seen this?" I handed her the flyer. I sucked in my breath and pointed to her picture.

"They couldn't have picked a better picture? I don't even let my boyfriend see me without make up on."

"That's your biggest concern?" I asked.

"Well, yeah." She shrugged and gave me back the flyer. "Don't really care who knows what I am."

"You do realize that people on this list have been turning up dead."

"I wouldn't worry about it. I have been trailing the group. It's only a matter of time before they screw up," Tom said matter-of-factly as he filled up his plate with baked goods.

"You know who the leader is?" I asked.

"Of course I do. Some of us don't rely on luck but skill to get the job done," Tom said with a smug smile.

"Well who is he?" I asked.

"Why should I tell you? I'm close to having enough evidence on him for an arrest. It's only a matter of time before I'm back on top," he said.

"I'm not looking for gold stars here. I want to be able to find out if they're connected to Trevor's murder," I said.

"Well then I will tell you after I make the arrest. The guy is dead; it's not like it's urgent," Tom said picking up one of the cookies from the basket. I read the sign in front of the basket:

Dream cookies: Warning Causes vivid dreams

Only to be used before sleep.

Don't eat more than one at a time.

"Tom don't eat …" I started to say.

"Why?" He asked.

"Oh, let him eat his cookie. He deserves it," Alice said.

"Alice, he doesn't know what …."

"Why you don't want him to have the cookie? Really Claire." Alice shook her head at me. "Do you just not like him that much?"

"You see what I have to put up with," Tom said popping three cookies into his mouth.

"Oh, Tom," I said shaking my head. I picked up the sign and showed it to him.

Tom didn't read it. He pushed my hand aside. "It's just a cookie. I'm not allergic to anything that could be in a cookie." He ate another cookie and walked away.

"Wicked girl," I said to Alice.

"Admit it you're loving it," she said.

"Maybe a little." I smiled and glanced at Tom. "If it doesn't kill him that is."

She laughed. "He reminds me of my father. Not in the good way. The cookies won't kill him. He may wish they'd kill him after it starts." I laughed. It felt good to laugh. Ever since Trevor died, I haven't felt much like laughing.

I went over and sat down next to my mom at the bar. She was drinking a cup of tea and talking to Sean.

"Where's Molly?" I asked.

"Trevor wanted to hear firsthand what people thought of him, so she and Trevor are making the rounds," Mom said.

"Well that's a little creepy," I said.

"At least they're enjoying themselves," Mom said. "It's nice to see so many people willing to come to a party for Trevor."

"Free beer always brings out the courage to overcome great burdens in life." Sean grinned, "It's how my wife would get me to the opera." He poured me a cup of coffee and placed it next to me.

"Where's Colin?" I asked.

"Where else?" Sean pointed with his eyes to the right. I turned my chair around and saw he was talking to Brittany. I nodded slightly and he patted my wrist, "You'll always be the prettiest girl in the room to me, darlin'."

"Thank you." I smiled. I would have loved to have seen what he was like in his youth. He must have been quite the ladies' man.

"Penguins," Tom squealed as he ran aimlessly around the room removing his clothes. I noticed that Tom had scars that ran along his chest and legs.

"What's that about?" Mom asked.

"No clue," Sean said. My mother caught me looking away and shook her head. The crowd went silent as we all watched Tom climb on to the table wearing nothing but his boxers and a sock on his left foot.

"Do something before they get us." Tom grabbed a fork and was stabbing the air "Penguins!" Everyone started to laugh, and a few people close to Tom took pictures with their phone. After a few minutes Colin and another man, I didn't recognize, took pity on Tom and dragged him off the table and into the back office.

Everyone froze when Tom entered the office the next morning. I watched him from the window of my office. To Tom's credit he held his head up high all the way there.

"Son of a bitch!" From the sound of it Tom was throwing a fit in his office. A wave of laugher erupted in the office. Curiosity got the better of me and I walked down to see what the fuss was about.

"Tom?" I knocked on the frame of his door.

"Did you come to gloat?" Tom asked.

"No why ... oh," Tom's office was littered with penguin paraphernalia from bobble heads to life-sized blow-up dolls. "I didn't know."

"Don't try to deny that you're not pleased with this turn of events," he said.

"No matter how much I don't like you, I will never be pleased with someone else's pain," I said.

"I'm sure your crying inside," he said.

"I was the one who tried to stop you from eating the cookies," I said.

"What do you want, Claire?" He said knocking the row of stuffed penguins that lined his desk into the trash bin.

"I was hoping you'd reconsider telling me how to find the leaders of the Brotherhood of Humanity group."

"I want credit if you catch anything."

I hadn't expected him to say yes. I stood there for a moment before saying, "You can take all the credit you want. I just want to protect my sister and everyone else that is on their hit list."

"I will have to clear it with Gail. I know she wouldn't let you go alone. She even makes me take someone," he scoffed. "Not that it'd do any good if they ever learned I was a Survivor. I'll call you as soon as I've talked to her."

He sat down at his desk, and started to look over a piece of paper. "You need to turn the knob and push, if the mechanics are preventing you from leaving my office."

I could barely contain my excitement while I waited for Tom's call. Evil genius that he is, my phone rang as I entered the ladies' room.

"Bring whomever is going with you to my office, I will go over everything in detail. The group is meeting tomorrow night."

"Thank you," I said. "We'll be there as soon as the detectives arrive."

"You know this doesn't mean I like you," he said.

"Oh, Tom, you know how to give a girl the warm and fuzzies," I said just before he hung up.

I called the detectives to ask them to stop by when they had time, because I had a lead on our cases. The detectives came in 15 minutes later. They must have used the lights and sirens. "So what's the big emergency?" Detective Moseley asked taking a seat across from my desk.

"I've been spending every moment I can trying to find out anything on the Brotherhood of Humanity group. The only way I see how we can get close enough to find anything out is by going to one of their meetings," I said.

"I'm sorry. Are you seriously thinking that you're going to walk into a meeting and they're going to admit to a room full of people their evil plans?" Detective Moseley snorted. "This isn't a Saturday morning cartoon."

"Ha ha. No," I grimaced and said, "I was planning on reading their minds." Detective Moseley's back stiffened and a visible tic started around his left eye.

"Oh, so we are all going?" Austin asked.

"Well, no. Tom was only able to get two of us in the meeting tonight," I said.

"I will go with you," Colin said.

"I don't think it would be a good idea for Colin to go with you," Austin said. "He was marked as one of the sympathizers along with his dad."

"I don't think anyone would make the connection," Colin said.

"Really? You don't think they'd recognize you?" Austin asked.

"Name one way they'd recognize me in a crowd full of people?"

"I can name three," Austin said. "One, you and your dad threw a party for Trevor's announcement on the news. Two, you had a wake for Trevor. And three, your dad has been way too public about his positive views of the Survivors."

"You make it sound like it's a bad thing. How do you

really feel about us?" Colin asked. Colin stood up and walked towards Austin.

"I have no problem with Survivors," Austin said.

"I think he's right," I said. They both turned to me. "You did have a confrontation not that long ago in the bar with two of their members. It might not be safe for you."

"Then who'd you take to replace me? That detective?" Colin asked pointing at Austin.

"Well I need someone to come with me. He can protect me. Or did you want me to go alone?" I asked.

"I'll go to the meeting with you," Austin said.

"Let's go talk to Tom, if there are no more objections?" I asked.

Hearing no objections, Austin and I walked down to Tom's office. I knocked on the door and he motioned us to come take a seat.

"Interesting pick," Tom said as he looked at Austin. "The meeting is tomorrow night at eight at a restaurant called 'A Little Slice of Heaven'." He handed me a piece of paper with the address of the restaurant. "The man running the meeting tomorrow night is Anthony Bianco, the owner of the restaurant and the son of, Richard Bianco, the leader of the group. Anthony wants to meet with both of you before the meeting at 7:00, to see if you qualify for the meeting."

"Qualify?" Austin asked raising an eyebrow.

"Yes, you must blend in well with them. They are very religious, so wear appropriate outfits and get your story straight before the meeting. Don't expose my identity to the group. I will be at the meeting; I use an alias, Gavin Jones."

"Thank you, Tom," I said.

"Don't screw this up," Tom said glaring at us.

"I'm guessing he's a close friend?" Austin asked as we left Tom's office.

"Oh yeah. We're just the best of friends," I said.

"I can't believe we are having our second date already," Austin said.

"It's not a real date. We're going to hunt for potential killers," I said.

"Well ... do we have to dress up?" Austin asked.

"Yes."

"Are we going to eat while there?"

"It's at a restaurant so I guess so."

"It sounds like a date to me, dinner and a show." He smiled at me and I laughed.

"All right can you pick me up around 6:30?" I asked.

"Yes. See you then." I was happy for the rest of the day despite Colin's refusal to talk to me.

CHAPTER NINETEEN

Austin pulled up to the curb right at 6:30. He shut off the engine and walked around the car. We both wore modest clothes, appropriate for church. I wore a simple knee length black skirt and a lavender sweater set that went nicely with my green eyes. Detective Austin wore a nice blue button-down shirt and khakis.

"Why didn't you wait for me to come up to the door?" Austin asked.

"I thought this would be faster. My mother and sister are home. We don't have time for an inquisition tonight," I said.

"I don't mind. I don't like the thought of you waiting outside at night," he said.

"This time it's more business than pleasure. I will try waiting for you in my apartment next time." He opened the door to the passenger side of the car and waited until I was safely in before returning to the driver's seat.

"So what's our story?" Austin asked.

"What story? I asked.

"You know how we met. What are we doing there? Stuff like that," he said.

I thought about it for a moment and said, "Oh, I guess we can just modify the truth."

"Modify the truth," he repeated with a chuckle. "That will work."

"What's so funny?" I asked.

"You just have a positive spin on everything. I always liked that about you. We both see the bad side of human nature every day," he said. "But you still see the good in people. Sometimes that's hard for me. You lighten what would otherwise be very grim days."

I blushed because he had just brightened my day. However, we were setting off on a potentially dangerous assignment so, I changed the subject to less personal small talk for the rest of the drive.

"A Little Slice of Heaven" was in the middle of a long street of businesses, on the other side of town. The restaurant's closed sign hung in the window and the door was locked so we knocked. A large man whose body looked like it was made from a ball of playdough opened the door and yelled, "Can't you read the sign? We're closed."

"We have an appointment to see Anthony Bianco before the meeting," I said stepping back.

"And you are?" He snorted.

"Claire and Austin," I said.

"Oh, come on in," he said as he started walking back into the restaurant. "A Little Slice of Haven", was a pizza parlor. Everything in the restaurant was colored red and black. Photos of famous celebrities from the twenties and thirties hung around the room.

We quickly followed as the heavyset man led us to a small office in the back of the restaurant. The office was filled with piles of folders and filing cabinets. We moved a small pile of folders off two chairs and placed them on what I assumed was a desk. When we sat down, the large man said, "Don't touch anything." He pointed a finger at Austin. "I will not be far," he pointed to his eye and then to Austin.

When he left, Austin asked, "Isn't he charming?"

"I'm just glad he wasn't Anthony," I said.

A man in his early thirties came striding into the room. "Sorry to keep you good folks waiting. I'm Anthony

Bianco. You must be Claire and Austin?"

"Yes," I said with a smile. "We don't mind waiting. We are just glad to be here."

"You won't be disappointed." Anthony rubbed a hand through his heavily shellacked black hair. "We've got a lot to celebrate tonight."

"What are you guys celebrating?" Austin asked.

"We're going to be celebrating the courageous young officer who killed our number one enemy." I listened to his thoughts; *I wish I had done it. Been the hero my dad would be proud of.*

"Oh, we heard of that on the news," Austin said while I remained quiet. "Did you guys know the young officer?"

"Yes, we sure did." He smiled. "We're generally not that friendly with law enforcement types but he was a special case. A real go getter. You guys must be pretty special, too. As you know, we don't let just anyone come to these events."

"We're very grateful that you're giving us this chance." I smiled. "Gavin has told us so much about you guys."

"Gavin is a fine young man." Anthony nodded. "Very dedicated to the cause."

"Oh yes, he is dedicated to the cause." Just not yours, I thought.

"Tell me a little about yourselves?" Anthony asked.

"Well we have been dating for a few months. I just graduated with a Master's in psychology and am trying to find my place in the world. I bet you can tell from his haircut that my honey here is a detective." Except for how long we'd been dating it was all true.

"You look too young to be out of college, let alone have a Master's degree," he said.

"I get that all the time." I smiled. "I'm only 24 but I was very motivated to graduate early and didn't spend a lot of time partying."

"What brings you two here?" He asked looking at Austin.

"We're both finding it hard to feel safe in the world with those people living all around us," I said shaking my head. "Found out that one of my cousins was hiding a dangerous side effect from me all these years. She's a telepath. It's just hard to trust anyone, so when Gavin told us about your group we were really excited to join." My hands started to shake. Austin placed his large warm hand over them and smiled.

"I'm very sorry to hear that. I've heard the same story from many of our members. So many families have been destroyed by this," Anthony said. His thoughts were of his sister that his father disowned after finding out she was a Survivor.

"I like what I see in you two. You guys sound like our type of people," he said. "You can stay for the meeting as guests, as long as you just stay back and observe. If everything goes well tonight and your background check clears, you can participate in the next meeting," he said. Anthony's thoughts reflected that I looked too sweet and innocent to be a Survivor, but he wasn't so sure about Austin. I stifled a laugh.

"Oh, we can do that, sir," Austin said. Anthony perked up at the word sir.

"I'm sure you will be full-time members in no time," He said. "The meeting is not for another half an hour but you're welcome to stay and have a bite to eat."

"Thank you, we will do that." We stood up and Anthony offered his hand. My hand felt slightly sticky after shaking his hand and I remembered the hair gel.

We both went and washed our hands, and then took a table near the window in the dining room. After some time an older woman came by, "What'll you have?"

"What do you have?" Austin asked.

She pointed to the pie pans showing the different sizes of pizza they carry. "Pizza."

We stared at each other. When the waitress cleared her throat, I said, "Pepperoni pizza and two sodas," I said hoping that was ok with Austin and if it wasn't he wouldn't say anything. Pizza topping preferences is something a normal couple would know about each other. She wrote it down and Austin said, "That sounds great." She left without saying a word.

The staff came in and out of the room setting up for the meeting by rearranging the tables and chairs. We stuck to casual topics just in case someone overheard.

We were doing pretty well but I was glad when the pizza came out so that we could stop looking for safe topics to talk about. When I reached for the pepper shaker at the end of the table, I noticed something moving outside the window. I moved closer to the window and tried to focus on the blurry image. I realized that it was Colin in his wolf form sitting across the street watching us. "Oh no," I whispered louder than I meant to. Luckily no one else was around.

"What is it?" Austin whispered. He leaned to look out the window. "I don't see anything."

"Colin is out there," I said keeping my voice low.

"Where? I don't see him."

"Let's just say it's not something you could see and leave it at that for now."

"Oh." I could see the light flashing in his eyes, as he understood what I was saying. "Why is he here?"

"I think he feels left out."

"I think he's jealous."

"No, not like that. We have been friends since as long as I can remember and partners at work for two years."

Austin finished off most of the pizza. I didn't feel much like eating. As Austin ate, the bouncer was letting people in and checking them off on his clipboard. He evicted us from the table with heavy breathing and a hand movement that indicated we had to leave after most of the chairs had been occupied. We moved to the back row of the seats facing the microphone and sat next to the window. I noticed Tom in the front row. I gave him a friendly wave and he gave his best attempt at a friendly wave back.

"Welcome, in honor of tonight's celebration, our leader has a few thoughts to share with us. Please turn off all cell phones and pagers at this time," Anthony said.

I hated to do it but I also didn't want to get us thrown out, so I turned off my cell phone. Richard Bianco stepped up to the microphone; he was a taller version of his son with slightly more hair.

"It's not natural to come back from the dead," Richard said into the microphone. I saw he was wearing a cross over his buttoned up white shirt. I wondered if he ever read the bible. I thought of mailing him a Cliff Notes version of the New Testament. What did he think we were celebrating at Easter?

"These diseased and mutated children of the dark are here to destroy the children of the light. We can be warriors of God. Like the good God-fearing man, Officer Olsson. We have already raised money to try and free him from his oppressors. But we must do more." Richard clutched his right hand over his heart and looked up to the ceiling. "We must stop them in God's name. We have the power!"

The crowed was clapping and swaying with the music that started from the keyboard player behind Richard. After Richard was done firing up the room, Anthony stepped back up to the microphone for the real business of the meeting. The only two items on tonight's agenda were a need for volunteers to draft and circulate a petition for a National Survivor Register and volunteers to run either a bake sale or car wash to raise bail money for Officer Olsson.

At the end of the meeting, everyone got up and milled around the snack tables set up around the room. I was hoping that we would be able to speak with Richard but after speaking with a few of his followers he stepped out to take a phone call.

Instead, I circulated the room, listening to their thoughts instead of their voices. Half the room was more than willing to take action in stopping and hurting the Survivors. The other half of the room was scared of the Survivors, but didn't want to harm them. I couldn't pick up any one thought of someone planning to hurt or kill a Survivor only the general willingness to let it happen.

As our path led us closer to the windows again, I noticed Colin outside moving his head to indicate to go outside. I sighed and said, "Honey, I need to go get something from the car. I will be right back."

"Sure." Austin's back stiffened. "Do you need me to come?"

"No, I think it's best if you stay here and circulate." I couldn't think of any plausible reason for both of us to leave and then come back.

He nodded and before I could start walking. "Don't you need the keys?" Austin asked.

"Oh yes, thank you." I took the keys and went outside. I could feel the anger rising when I got to Colin. I didn't know what was worse, his moody attitude or his assumption that I needed a chaperone for everything. But just before I approached him, he turned and led the way.

The chilly air wrapped around my body as I followed him, my footsteps echoing as my feet hit the pavement. When I reached Colin I asked, "So?" He walked a few feet and stopped. He pointed his head down an alley. As I started walking down the side street, I felt something creeping in me. It was so faint that it took a moment to realize that it was fear.

I heard something. I stopped to listen. It sounded like a large metal trash bin falling over. I started walking faster down the side street towards the noise. Colin stepped in front of me trying to prevent me from going any farther.

"What's wrong?" I asked. I heard a cry. An image flashed in my mind of what looked like the trunk of a car being opened. I could tell it was a man's thoughts because I could see his large hands bound in plastic cuffs. I ran as fast as I could to the parking lot. I saw another image in my mind of the man being stabbed in the chest with a large butcher knife.

I searched down the rows of cars and trucks. When I reached the back of the lot, I saw a hand lying in a small puddle underneath a street lamp. The rest of his body must be hidden behind the red truck. "Who's there?" My voice squeaked.

The hand didn't move. Instead I saw a silhouette of a man rise from behind the truck. He stepped into the light of the street light and I could see it was Richard. He grinned at me waving a large butcher knife in his hand.

I started to walk backwards. He was walking towards me whistling as he twirled the knife. I scanned the parking lot looking for another way out. It was walled in with a fence, and the only exit was behind me.

"Colin?" I screamed down the side street. Before I could scream again, he was on me. Richard's leather glove covered my mouth and nose. I managed to hit his hand hard enough to drop the knife. He grabbed the back of my shirt and slammed me against the hood of the car I was standing next to. It felt like someone had taken a bat to my ribcage.

"I'm going to enjoy this." Richard grabbed my left wrist and twisted up and hit it against the fence. I heard a crack in my wrist. It felt like tiny pieces of glass were flowing through the veins of my wrist and hand. He hit me twice in the face and then slammed me against the fence. My breathing started to slow down as he covered my mouth and nose. I heard a noise from behind me. He let go of me. My legs felt weak, they couldn't hold me up, so I dropped to the wet concrete. I saw him pick up the knife. I heard footsteps. "Till next time," Richard said pulling himself over the wooden fence.

Everything hurt. I lay there on the concrete not wanting to move. I saw Austin running down the side street. "Claire? Are you ok? Who did this?"

"Richard. He went over the fence." Austin helped me to my feet. The pain surged through my body. "How did you know I was out here?"

"Colin called me." He gently touched my bruised

cheekbone. My body flinched like he was hitting me. "Why did you come back here alone? I wasn't that far away."

"Oh no." I started walking towards the back of the parking lot. He followed me. "I saw him dying." We both looked down at the man lying in the puddle of blood. Next to his head was a poster held down by a rock. I bent down and recognized him as Bill Mason, Trevor's lab assistant, the one who had gone on the news with him the night he went public with his research.

"Are you sure it was Richard Bianco who attacked you?" Austin asked. I looked over my shoulder; Austin was using a flashlight to look into the driver's seat of a red ford truck.

"Yes. It's not something I could mix up."

"I think you should come look at this." I walked over cradling my arm next to my chest. I had a hard time seeing in the truck since I was shorter than the window. I stepped on the running board. I fell backwards when I saw it was Richard slumped over the steering wheel of the truck. Austin caught me before I hit the ground.

Before I passed out I thought, well, I guess we were wrong. We aren't looking for a group of people out to kill Survivors. We are looking for a serial killer who is a Survivor.

THE PUZZLE KEEPER

CHAPTER TWENTY

I went in and out of consciousness for what seemed like hours. The pain and nausea were the only things that let me know the difference between dreaming and being awake.

The sound of beeping dragged me back to reality. My eyes felt sore, and the light of the room burned like acid.

I was unable to focus on the person above me, but I knew it was my mother. She had a distinctive smell of apples and cinnamon.

"Just five more minutes." I closed my eyes.

"You're not late for work, Claire," Mom said.

"Do you remember what happened?" A male voice asked, bringing me fully conscious. I looked around the room and realized it was Colin who had asked the question. The sharp pain that hit me the moment I tried to sit reminded me of what had happened.

"I remember." A cold breeze on my naked skin made me all too aware that I had on just a flimsy hospital gown. I brought the blanket that was on my lap to my neck and sat back on the hospital bed. My brain tingled, it was hard to think straight, but I managed to ask, "What happened?"

My mother spoke before he could, "No. None of that. We're not going to talk about that tonight. Not now."

"You're right, it can wait," Colin said.

I smiled at Colin as much as the pain would let me. He winced looking at my face.

After several x-rays and a shot of morphine, a tall Asian doctor came in the room.

"Hello again, Claire, I'm Dr. Lee," the doctor said. I didn't remember him but that wasn't saying much. "How are you doing?"

"Well if I don't move or breathe, I'm doing pretty good," I said.

"I'm afraid, that's to be expected. Well I do have some good news for you," Dr. Lee said.

"Yeah? What would that be?" I asked.

"Well you only have a broken wrist, bruised ribs and some minor bruising around your face and neck," Dr. Lee said with a smile.

"Wow, that does sound like good news," I said. I wondered what he considered to be bad news.

"Doesn't it?" Dr. Lee was smiling a bit too cheerfully for a doctor dealing with patients in the emergency room.

"I was being sarcastic. How could that possibly be good news?" I asked.

"The good news is you don't need surgery and you don't need to stay in the hospital tonight. To be honest we were worried with how you looked that the injuries were far worse." I was now glad I had avoided all mirrors since I got to the hospital.

"I guess that is good news," I moaned as the blanket brushed my chest. "So I can go back to work tomorrow?"

"That pain must be making you a bit delusional," Dr. Lee said.

"No I'm afraid that's normal for her," my mother said.

"Yes. I see." Dr. Lee nodded. "If work's a problem I can write you a note. You really should be resting at home for the next few days. It's not like the world's going to end if you take a few days off."

"Don't worry. She will be taking the next few days off." My mother said putting her hand up when I tried to talk.

"It's really important that I go back to work. Before

who did this," I pointed with my good hand to my face, "finds me or Molly and finishes what he started."

"Well you're not a child so I can't force you to stay home," Dr. Lee said.

"It doesn't matter her age. She's my child. She will be staying at home," Mom said.

"There are plenty of other people able to find the man who did this to you," Colin agreed. "I'll make sure you're safe." I nodded as much as I could. The thought of staying home while a serial killer was out there hunting made me shiver. However, at the moment I didn't have much of a choice, I knew it was a losing battle once they joined forces. I'd have to wait until I had a bit more energy.

"I'm sure you're in good hands," Dr, Lee said. "I'm going to get a nurse to give you another shot of pain medication then bring you to the casting room to have your left wrist put in a cast and put your arm in a sling. After that you can pick up your pain medication and go home."

I smiled at the words "go home". I'd pay a hundred dollars just to have a chance to have a hot shower to rinse off the twigs and dirty water still in my hair. "You know what? I was wrong. That does sound like good news."

CHAPTER TWENTY-ONE

They must have gotten me home, because the next thing I remember was waking up in my bed with Colin sleeping on the computer chair that sat in the corner of my room. My mother was sitting next to my bed knitting a purple baby blanket. When I tried to sit up, I realized that I couldn't because Rosie was sleeping on my feet.

"Good to see you up," Mom said putting down her knitting and moving to sit on my bed.

I looked at Colin. "Was he here all night?"

She nodded, "And all day. You were asleep most of the day. He didn't fall asleep until about an hour ago."

I let out a moan with every inch of progress I made sitting up.

"Do you need something?" Colin jumped up from the chair. I gripped my left wrist that was now covered in a pink cast. Colin came to my bedside with a pill and handed me a glass of water that sat on the small table next to my bed.

"Thank you," I said.

"You must be hungry. I'll go make some pancakes." Mom bent down and kissed my forehead. Colin took her place on my bed after she left.

"You know I didn't mean for you to get hurt," his eyes met mine, searching for a response.

I finished my glass of water and put it on the table. "Why did you want me to come out with you if something like that was happening?" I asked.

"I saw Richard when he came out of the restaurant. He walked to the back lot, talking on his phone. I wanted to follow him but didn't want to leave you. After a long time had passed and he hadn't come back, I went to the parking lot. He was easy to find. Large puffs of cigarette smoke came from one of the trucks. It was too dark and I was too short to see into the truck, but from their voices I knew Richard was in the truck talking to another man. I couldn't see the other man but I could pick up on part of their conversation. From the snippets I could hear, they were talking about adding someone to the list. I was hoping you could read their minds. So it wouldn't happen."

"Why didn't you just call me?" I asked. "I could have brought Austin with me."

"I saw you turn your phone off before the meeting. I didn't think I had the time to get there in person; my body was back at my place. I panicked," Colin said.

"Oh, yeah, I forgot about that," I said.

"I honestly thought you would have brought Austin out with you," Colin said.

"If we both came out, we wouldn't be able to go back in and we still hadn't talked to Richard," I said.

Colin nodded. After a moment he said, "Once we headed to the back lot, I smelled death and tried to stop you."

"How could you think I would stop if there was still a chance I could have saved him?" I asked.

"I never want to be that close to losing you," Colin said looking down at me. I put my hand on his arm.

"Pancakes are ready," my mother called from outside the room. We pulled away from each other.

"Lucky you," Colin snickered. "I wonder what kind they are."

"Based on last week, it's probably a South American version of pancakes ... and I wouldn't laugh. You know she made enough for you, too." Colin swallowed his laugh and looked at the door.

CHAPTER TWENTY-TWO

I spent the next three days resting at home. Except for when I needed the bathroom or a shower, Colin, my mother or Molly stayed within feet of me. I was getting ready for another fun-filled evening of watching old reruns on TV, when my mother informed me that I had visitors. Visitors had been stopping by for the last three days, but my mother shooed them away, thinking the excitement might kill me.

After brushing my hair and exchanging my pink sweats for a tank top and jeans, I went out into the living room. I found Austin and Detective Moseley sitting on the sofa. Molly was talking to them when I walked in the room. Austin's cheeks grew red and I realized she was grilling him about how I got hurt when I was with him. Austin stood up when he saw me. "How are you feeling?"

"I'm much better. I can breathe without crying," I said with a smile. From the looks on everyone else's face apparently I was the only one who thought it was funny.

"I'm glad you're feeling better. Did you get my flowers?" Austin looked around the room. Between Molly and me, we received so many flowers our living room looked like a small florist shop.

"Yes, thank you very much. I moved yours to my bedroom," I said with a smile, remembering the pink lilies next to my bed.

"Molly, can you come help me fold the laundry?" Mom

asked from the hallway.

"Just leave it. I'll do it later," Molly said.

"Molly?" Mom said firmly.

"Coming." We watched Molly disappear into the hallway. I sat in Molly's seat and Colin moved a dining room chair to sit next to me.

"How's the investigation coming?" I asked.

"That's why we're here. I didn't want you to find out from the news. We arrested someone for the murder," Austin coughed.

"Who?" Colin asked.

"Richard Bianco." Austin turned his body to look at me. "I know you don't think he did it." I was about to say something but he put his hand up. "I don't either. But there's just too much evidence against him. We have fingerprints, a room full of witnesses that saw him leave the restaurant just before the murder and we found him near the victim at the time of the attack."

"But I saw the murder. I know it wasn't him. Doesn't that count for something?" My chest hurt as my breathing increased. Maybe I wasn't up for this much excitement.

"Well ... technically you said it was Richard who killed Bill Mason and was your attacker," Austin said.

"Yeah, he did look exactly like him but he couldn't be him. Richard was in the car unconscious when the killer went over the fence. I saw it with my own eyes. How can you explain that?" I asked.

"Maybe you just don't remember," Detective Moseley said. "It was dark outside, and you were injured pretty bad."

"I know what I saw," I said.

"Are you seriously thinking there is a man who looks exactly like Richard just wandering around?" Detective Moseley asked.

"No, I think there is one man who has committed all of our murders and who knows how many others." Everyone looked at me as if I was crazy, so I added, "If you think about it none of the murderers remember the crime. The victims were all killed in the same way. All had a poster at the crime scene."

"Even if that's true. How could one man do it all?" Austin asked.

"It's got to be a Survivor," I said.

"You think there's a Survivor out there with the ability to shapeshift?" Detective Moseley asked.

"I guess that's a possibility. Maybe the killer has an ability that allows him to disguise himself. Who knows what other abilities are out there," Colin said.

"That's just ridiculous," Detective Moseley said. "Why would anyone do that?"

"Ah, but that's the thing," I cradled my injured arm to my chest. "For every murder, he has two victims: the person he murders and the person who goes to jail. I thought about the four people charged for each crime. They all have one thing in common, in some way each of them have expressed hatred for the Survivors."

"How would the killer know that those people felt that way about the Survivors?" Austin asked.

"It'd be easy. Except for Nadine they all took part in the Brotherhood of Humanity group," Colin said.

"I can understand a Survivor targeting the men who did the crime. But why kill the Survivors?" Austin asked.

"That I can't figure out," I said.

"Could be the person is trying to start a conflict between the Survivors and non-Survivors," Detective Moseley said.

"We need to find out how he picks his victims, and who the real targets are, before he kills again," Colin said.

"So the big question is, if you're right, how do we catch a person who can look like anyone?" Austin asked.

My mother took our silence as a cue to come back into the room. She looked at our faces, "Bad news?"

"Just thinking, Mom," I said, when no one else answered.

"Well, dinner should be ready soon," Mom said. She glanced at the detectives and added, "There's plenty, if you detectives would like to stay."

"What's for dinner?" I asked before the detectives could answer.

"I think Molly has a lasagna in the oven," Mom said. "To be honest she hasn't let me in the kitchen. You know how she is about people helping her cook."

"I do." In this case, I agreed with Molly.

"I'd be delighted to stay for dinner, Mrs. Bennett," Austin said.

"So would I, I have lived off drive through burgers and tacos for longer than I care to remember," Detective Moseley said with a smile. When he caught my eyes lingering over him, he cleared his throat and quickly pulled the corners of his lips down.

"Maybe I should make a side dish since so many people are staying," Mom said.

"There is no need to go to the extra trouble, Mom. I have a salad to go with it," Molly said from the kitchen.

"I guess that's enough food. What about a dessert?" Mom asked.

Molly rummaged through the fridge. After a few moments of clinking dishes and heavy sighs, Molly looked through the opening in the kitchen and said, "Afraid we don't have anything."

"I can go downstairs and grab something from the bakery," Colin said standing up and heading towards the door.

"Don't be silly. The detectives were looking forward to a homemade dinner. I'll just whip up some exotic cupcakes. Maybe seaweed or lavender," Mom said with a smile.

"Try a normal cupcake, Mom. Our guests might not like exotic."

"No, no cupcakes, Mom," Molly said. "You can't use the oven; the lasagna is in there."

I didn't think she heard me over Molly's loud voice because she ignored my question and said, "That's fine. I will put them in after you take out the lasagna. It will be cooked and ready to eat by the time dinner is over."

"Don't go to any trouble for us. We are just happy to eat a nice dinner," Austin said.

"No trouble at all. I love to cook," Mom said.

After Mom went into the kitchen to help with dinner, Colin said, "You might want to find a polite way of turning down the cupcakes – like filling up on lasagna."

"Why? Is she a bad cook?" Detective Moseley asked.

"She likes to incorporate recipes she has learned on her trips. Sometimes the food is fabulous, other times I'm glad I have a dog that eats anything," I said, scratching the top of Rosie's head.

As we sat down to the table, Mom announced that she had just popped the cupcakes in the oven.

"Wonderful," I said with a smile. We were all pretty quiet the first few minutes giving our undivided attention to Molly's lasagna. I was hoping that Mom would stay distracted and not interrogate the detectives but it was not to be.

"Well, Detective Moseley, have you been a detective long?" My mother asked pouring herself a glass of wine.

"Four years, though it seems like longer," Detective Moseley said.

"Did you always want to be a detective?" She indicated with her eyes his empty wine glass.

"Yes, Ma'am. Joined the academy as soon as I was old enough," he said, picking up the wine glass and holding it near her.

"It's rare to find someone so young who is passionate for their job and knows exactly what they want to do," Mom said pouring the wine. Mom looked at his hand, and said, "I notice you're missing a ring, are you separated or widowed?"

"Mom!" Molly and I said in unison. We all dropped our forks and looked between Detective Moseley and my mother.

"It's all right," he reassured us. "I'm separated."

"I didn't know that," Austin said. "Why didn't you tell

me?"

"Didn't really matter. I only really care about my daughter Daisy."

"That has to be hard," Molly said, putting a hand on her stomach.

"It is. My Ex has custody at the moment, but I'm confident that will change very soon." Detective Moseley smiled. His voice and face softened when he talked about his daughter; I was seeing a different side of him now.

"I hope that happens for you soon. I couldn't imagine raising a child alone," Molly said.

"Um, I thought …" Detective Moseley started to say.

"Oh, no Trevor is still around. In fact, he is sitting on the couch," Molly smiled.

There was utter silence at the table until I said, "Her side effect allows her to see and hear ghosts."

Mom changed the subject by asking Austin, "So I heard that you went out with my daughter the other night."

"Yes, Ma'am," Austin said. "I have wanted to for a long time. Your daughter is one of the most upbeat and caring women I know." Austin reached for my hand under the table and squeezed it. I wondered if the room was warming up or if I was blushing as I squeezed his hand back.

"How long have you known each other?" My mother asked.

"It's been about two years," Austin said.

"It took you two years to ask her out?" Mom asked.

"I was under the impression that Claire was dating Colin. I misread their closeness as romantic instead of friendship. When I caught Colin looking at a young lady, I asked him if he was dating Claire. When he told me no, I asked her out the next chance I had."

Molly looked at our Mom and they both immediately started to laugh.

"What's so funny?" Colin asked.

"You two dating." Their laughter grew louder and Rosie started pacing around them barking.

"I fail to see the humor," Colin said.

"Please, the way you two bicker?" Molly commented.

"Besides, you date a new party girl in her early twenties every month. You rarely remember their last names," Mom said.

"What's wrong with a little variety?" Colin said.

"For you, that's just fine. I'm just happy Claire is dating a good man," Mom said coming out of the kitchen with a small plate of dark pink cupcakes and light pink frosting.

"They look delicious, Mrs. Bennett," Austin said, picking up one of the cupcakes.

"Thank you. I hope they turned out ok," Mom said.

Austin took a bite of his cupcake. We all watched for his reaction, as if he was a poison tester.

"This is delightful. I hope there's enough for two," he said with a smile.

"Oh, you're so kind. I think you're in luck. I made enough for everyone to have four," Mom said.

I didn't see Austin flinch or gag after he finished his cupcake, so I picked up a cupcake from the center of the table. I sniffed the cupcake; it smelled like mint. I took off the wrapper and looked at the cupcake from every angle, it looked normal so I took a bite of it. It was mint all right but it tasted like eating an entire tube of toothpaste.

"How much peppermint did you put in this, Mom?" Molly asked.

"You know I don't use measuring cups. I just poured what looked right."

"Not many people can cook without using measuring cups," Austin said.

"Thirteen years ago, I would have thought it was crazy to cook without measuring spoons and cups. But I was forced to cook that way, when I went to remote areas for my job. I found cooking that way is more creative and I have a real passion for cooking creatively now," Mom said.

"Coincidently, Molly also discovered a passion for cooking around the same time but she sticks to recipes and measuring," I said.

The detectives excused themselves and left shortly after the too minty cupcakes. Austin, bless his heart, saved the rest of us by asking if he could take the cupcakes to some deserving new recruits at the police station.

CHAPTER TWENTY-THREE

The next morning, Colin had to return to work. After much arguing, he agreed to drive me into the office, mostly because the thought of me staying home alone made him more nervous than me overdoing it. At first, Gail tried to send me home but then she capitulated, and had a small sofa from the waiting room brought to our office for me to use when I got tired.

I told my story to everyone who saw me. I found my co-workers divided on their reactions to what happened to me. Half thought that I was brave. Somehow the case made them feel validated for risking so much for their jobs. The other half were scared, wondering if it was too late to quit and move to some remote location. Normally, I would try to convince them not to be scared, that someone had to protect the Survivors, but I couldn't when I felt the same way. I couldn't close my eyes without seeing his face grinning at me.

I spent the better part of the afternoon combing through the files on the murders that Detective Moseley had dropped off at lunch. I compared every aspect of the victims' lives, except for Susanna Russo whom we still knew nothing about. Nothing came of it; they all lived completely different lives. They went to different colleges, lived in different areas; they didn't even use the same grocery store. The only slight similarity was that they all knew Trevor.

With all the Survivors Trevor met doing research that was a pretty big victim pool.

The phone rang underneath the stacks of paper on my desk. I fished the phone out and saw it was Alice.

"Alice, Is everything all right?" I asked.

"Heya Claire. Everything's fine. I just wanted to let you know that I found Rosie wandering out in front of the bakery. I managed to get her in the bakery before anything happened."

"Thank you for getting her," I said letting out a sigh of relief. "I'm so sorry. I have no idea how she got out."

"I don't either. I went up and knocked but no one was home," Alice said. I knew Molly was out with some nurses she worked with to share her news about the baby and do a little shopping. Mom had gone to the University to touch base with her colleagues.

"We'll be there soon to pick Rosie up," I said.

On our way home, I noticed that several shops on the streets near the bakery were closed even though it was the middle of the day. I was feeling tense and a bit guilty for somehow letting Rosie outside. It all went away when I saw Rosie, getting a belly rub from a small freckled boy while an older girl dropped treats in her mouth. It must be tough being a dog.

"Has she been much trouble?" I asked.

"No, not at all," Alice replied. "She's increased business. I may have to buy a dog for the bakery. We sure need any extra help we can get with all the closed shops."

"Why so many?" Colin asked.

"Apparently this is becoming Survivor central. All the shops not run by Survivors have moved. Though new owners are moving in soon."

"That'll be interesting," Colin said. "I wonder what shops they'll put in."

We bought a few sugar cookies in the shape of white rabbits, and took Rosie home. Colin followed me to the front door of my apartment.

"Thanks, for driving me home," I said hoping he would take the hint.

"No problem," Colin said. He wasn't leaving. I sighed and just as I was going to grip the doorknob to slide my key in I noticed it moved with ease. I pushed the door a little and it opened.

"Did you lock the door?" He asked.

"No, I thought after being attacked by a stranger it would be easier to just leave the door unlocked for him." I rolled my eyes. "Of course, I did." He used his left arm to push me back, while he opened the door.

"Oh my," I said as I saw every spot on the wall covered in posters, the same poster. We leaned in and saw it was the *Top Twenty Most Dangerous Survivors* poster from the Brotherhood of Humanity group. However, we noticed something was different from the last time we had seen the poster. Trevor, Mrs. Cooper and Bill Mason still had a red "x" through their picture but now one picture had three circles around it like a bull's-eye, my picture.

We called the police and they responded within minutes. Austin must have heard it over the radio because he and Detective Moseley weren't far behind the officers. They walked the scene and took down my information.

"Do you have somewhere else you can stay?" Austin asked.

"Nowhere that I'd be any less vulnerable than I am here," I said.

"We don't have the budget for police protection. There are just too many Survivors that need protection. We are already stretched too thin protecting the high-profile Survivors, but we'd be willing to help watch your apartment at night," Austin said indicating himself and Detective Moseley.

I didn't know if I should laugh or cry. "Police protection didn't help Trevor."

"Would you rather stay in jail or leave the state?" Detective Moseley asked.

"You could stay at the Haven at work," Colin said. Austin nodded in agreement. "You could bring Molly and your mom."

"You want a telepath to sleep in a room full of anxiety-ridden strangers?" I asked.

"Just for tonight. If it doesn't work out we will figure out something else," Colin said.

I looked up at the posters and sighed, "Just for tonight."

CHAPTER TWENTY-FOUR

It took a few hours to locate Mom and Molly and get all three of us packed. We didn't reach the Survivor Haven until 10:00 pm. Abby was waiting for us just inside the door.

"Welcome to the Survivors' Haven," Abby said as she bent down and scratched the top of Rosie's head. "Too cute. Hi, Claire." Abby looked at Molly and then my mother. "You must be Claire's mom and sister." Molly and my mother glanced at me with a questioning expression. I shrugged, I didn't know if I told her about them or not.

"Oh, no I'm not reading your minds," Abby giggled. "I've seen your pictures in Claire's office."

"It's nice to meet you," my mother said shaking Abby's hand.

"I have your cots set up in the back," Abby said.

"Thanks for making room for us on such short notice," Molly said as we followed Abby down a row of cots.

"No problem at all. Claire tells me you're a nurse," Abby said.

I shook my head at Molly. It was a trap and I knew it. Molly ignored me and told her anyway, "Yes, I am."

"I was wondering. If you have the time, would you mind checking on some of the kids? We're a bit short staffed as I'm sure you've noticed. Many of the kids have minor injuries, but we don't have anyone qualified to take care of them. We don't even have enough staff to bring them to the doctor. Even if we did many of them are too terrified to leave this building."

Molly looked at me and I threw my arms up. She sighed. "I'd be more than happy to help out."

"Wonderful. Well this is your new home away from home." She indicated three cots with clean linens stacked on top of them. "Come and see me when you get settled," Abby said.

"Oh, you mean now?" It was late; about half the room was already asleep. Poor Molly, she tired easily these days between recovering from her wounds and being pregnant.

"Well if you don't mind."

"I will be there in a minute," Molly said. Abby scratched Rosie's head one more time and left.

"Thanks for the warning," Molly said grabbing a package of saltine crackers out of her bag.

"I tried. Did you not see my head shake?" I asked.

"I guess it wouldn't hurt. I'm just tired." I hugged her before she left to follow Abby.

"I'm sorry about this, Mom," I said, as we both made all three cots with the linens they had given us.

"About what dear?" Mom asked.

"Sleeping in a room full of strangers? Having a serial killer out stalking us? Having to give up work to come home?"

"It's no less dangerous than my work normally is," she said.

"That's really comforting to hear, Mom." I knew she was being honest. I spent time with her on some of her more tame travels, that in my opinion were well out of the realm of safe. My mother was both accident prone and fond of traveling to dangerous places to study culture and anthropology, not a safe combination.

"I wouldn't lie to you. Anyway, I think of this as an adventure," she said.

"I have been traveling the country hunting killers for the past two years, I don't think I really need more adventure," I said.

"You must enjoy it on some level. After you graduated from college you could have gotten a safe job. Become a therapist or something else mundane. As much as you try to deny it, I think you're just like me. You live for the puzzle, for the adventure."

"I do love puzzles." In fact, she was right. I was working on a puzzle with a few missing pieces, and I just couldn't think of anything but finding them.

"I'm always right." She smiled at me. "It's one of the perks to being a mother."

I laid down on my cot; it felt as comfortable as a pile of wet dirt with a rock as a pillow. Normally, I didn't mind roughing it. I had gone camping with my mom all over the world, and enjoyed every minute of it. But my chest and arm still ached with any type of pressure. "I wish the adventure came with better living conditions like a hotel with room service."

"This is like a luxury hotel compared to what I'm used to on my trips. Anyway, what kind of adventure comes with a hotel and room service?"

"Right now, my type of adventure." I squirmed around trying to find a comfortable spot. I thought of asking her what type of adventure she was on in a secure government building, but I was fairly confident that I didn't want to know.

Mom was asleep by the time Molly came back. Molly's body sagged as she sat on her cot.

"Are you ok?" I asked sitting up on my cot.

"Better than these kids." She rubbed her hands over her bloodshot eyes. "They're so scared. They have bruises and cuts. I have seen them on kids before, but this is just...."

"I'm sorry." I put my hand on her wrist.

"If you want, I can tell Abby that this is simply too much for you. You're pregnant and recovering from an injury, no one will blame you."

"No, I want to. I feel like I need to help them. I kept

looking at them, hearing what they've been through. I could have been any one of them." I sat next to her on her cot and pulled her into a hug. "I just don't know why out of all the children who lost parents, she picked me to save."

"You became part of the family the moment they put you next to me in the hospital. You didn't just need us. We needed each other."

It didn't take long for her to fall asleep. I, on the other hand, couldn't even doze. My eyes stung and I was becoming increasingly nauseous from being kept awake from the chatter. There was about a hundred people sleeping in the room, no one was awake, but their dreams streamed through me. I could have tried blocking their dreams, but I was simply too tired.

A little after one a.m. I took my lumpy pillow and flimsy white cotton blanket and left the Haven. Rosie followed me as I searched the floors for somewhere quiet to sleep, but the first available place I found was my office. I locked the door and checked it twice, before stretching out on the small sofa. It was warm, fluffy and quiet, my body relaxed immediately. I didn't even remember hitting the pillow before falling asleep.

I woke up in the middle of a dream with a jolt, with a sudden realization. I knew how the killer was picking the victims. I wrote down a few words to remind myself in the morning and happily went back to sleep.

"What are you doing sleeping in the office?" Colin was bending over me. If I ignore him maybe he will go away. "I know you're awake, you don't smile like that in your sleep."

"Fine, I'm up." Rosie jumped up on the sofa when I sat up and put her head in my lap. I stroked her head.

"The whole point of you sleeping here is so you can stay with everyone else in the Haven to be protected," Colin said.

"I couldn't sleep there. I figured I'd be safe in the office. I had Rosie with me," I said.

"Great, because she did such a good job protecting the apartment."

"We don't know what happened there. Anyway, I'm in a big government building, I think I'm pretty safe."

"That would be true if it wasn't for the fact that the killer can disguise himself as anyone. The killer could have just waltzed in here and killed you."

"I can't stay awake for days to stay safe."

He nodded. "I can stay with you tonight at your apartment."

"You need your sleep, too."

"We can take turns sleeping."

"Ok, we can see how it goes."

I stretched and walked to the white board with the clues of the Survivors on it. "I figured out how the killer is picking his victims. It's his research."

"What?" He asked.

"All three victims played a key role in Trevor's research."

"All of them?"

"Yes, Mrs. Cooper backed his research financially, Trevor did the research and Bill Mason was his assistant. I've been wracking my brain about what made Molly different; she is a Survivor after all. Now I get it. Molly never helped Trevor with his research. That's what made her different, that's why she didn't die."

"What about Susanna Russo?"

"We don't know enough about her to know whether or not she is part of this pattern. There were differences in the way she was attacked so maybe she isn't."

"That makes sense. You go get dressed before too many people see you." He indicated my pink monkey print PJ bottoms and banana yellow tank top. "I'll call the detectives with your theory."

CHAPTER TWENTY-FIVE

The Haven had already been set up for daytime activities. The sofas and comfortable chairs that had been moved to the walls were now scattered in the room. The children sat at different tables with one adult. After passing by one of the tables I realized the children had been separated by age and the adult was teaching them the multiplication tables. I guess I shouldn't have been surprised that the children were too afraid to go to school.

I saw Molly was in one of the glass offices. I knocked on the doorframe and stepped into the room.

"Morning, Claire," Molly said. "Glad to see you. We were worried when we woke up and you weren't on your cot."

"Sorry about that. Couldn't sleep." I noticed a plastic bucket that hospitals used for queasy patients, and a half-empty box of saltine crackers on top of the desk in front of her. "Speaking of worried. How are you?"

"Better," Molly smiled. "I'm just a little tired."

"Don't push yourself. It's not worth it," I said.

"Claire ..." Molly stopped talking when we heard a scream coming from the next room. We ran out of the office to see people starting to gather around a group of children who were sitting on the floor screaming. Molly bent down to one of the screaming children - a brown haired boy that was covering his ears with his hands. She looked at me. "I can't say no. Who else would help them?"

A sudden wave of images of a house on fire flowed through me. My body fought for air and quivered as the feeling of terror started to build inside me. Molly's scream brought me back.

Everyone near me was on the ground screaming. It must be one of the kids projecting their thoughts and emotions, but who? Another wave was coming, I closed my eyes and blocked the images with all the energy I had. When the wave stopped and the scream died down to whimpering, I ran my hands over the shirt sleeves of each of the children. I stopped at a girl around the age of six, with curly black hair. I could feel the raw emotions pouring off of her. I picked her up. Her whole body shivered as if she was cold. The wave was coming again. I ran. I made it to the hallway just before the next wave started.

"I'm sorry," the little girl whispered. I held her close and told her it would be ok. A few minutes later, Abby came rushing in from the elevator. She took the girl from my arms. A calming emotion radiated from Abby, into the little girl. Her panic died down, and she fell asleep in Abby's arms.

Abby carried the little girl to one of the glass offices in the Haven. "Can you get that?" She indicated the cot stacked against the wall.

I put the cot on the floor and she put the girl on the cot. "Is she going to be ok?" I asked.

"Yes, Beth will be fine she just needs some sleep."

"What about when it happens again?" I looked out the window at all the children in the room.

"I'll keep her with me. I can help her stop projecting the images and emotions," she said. "She was home when her house was set on fire. She's just having a hard time dealing with it," she said.

"How do you do that?" I asked.

"What?" she asked.

"Project your feelings onto someone else," I said.

"You have to block everyone's thoughts and feelings. I always picture myself in a bubble. Once that happens I build whatever emotion I want to project. I let my guard down a little when it's really strong like I'm going to burst and let it radiate out of me. Sometimes it helps to picture it happening like little sun rays coming from your fingertips," she said.

"That must be draining," I said. Just blocking people's thoughts was draining for me at times.

"If you do it enough it's no work at all. Projecting becomes as easy as reading feelings off people," she said.

Molly knocked on the doorframe. "How is she doing?"

"She'll be fine. But it wouldn't hurt to look her over."

I took that as a cue to leave. I hugged Molly on my way out. I would have waved to Abby but she was already preoccupied with Beth.

By the time I took a shower and changed, the detectives had already made it to our office.

Austin put the file he was reading down when he saw me. "It's good to see you, Claire."

He hesitated before giving me a hug. I could read from his thoughts that he had been worried all night, wondering if it was too soon in the relationship to be calling to check on me. "How was your night in the Haven?"

"I, uh … " I started to say.

"She didn't sleep there. She slept in the office," Colin said.

"But the point was to keep you around other people for your safety," Austin said.

"I know, but I can't sleep when there are so many people in the room," I said.

"I've already offered to stay with you at your apartment," Colin said.

"You can't give up your life like that – we don't know how long it will take to catch this guy," I said.

"Why don't Colin and I split the time watching over you?" Austin asked.

"We'll see. Why don't we concentrate on catching the killer so neither one of you will have to watch me?" I asked. I explained my theory on how the killer is picking his victims.

"Good work, Claire," Austin said.

"Are you sure about this?" Detective Moseley asked. "He could have just not killed Molly because she was pregnant."

"Molly didn't tell the killer that she was pregnant and as far as I can tell her stomach isn't showing," I said.

"I think she has a point," Colin said. "It would explain why the killer murdered Mrs. Cooper who is not a Survivor and didn't try to murder her son who is a Survivor."

"Let's suppose that the killer is killing anyone who was involved in Trevor's research, how did the killer find out who worked with Trevor?" Austin asked.

"Anyone who watched the news knew that Trevor and Bill Mason worked on the research. The only issue is how the killer knew about Mrs. Cooper," Colin said.

"I talked to Trevor about that before he died. He said that Mrs. Cooper was mentioned on his website."

"So the victims might be plausible, but what's the connection with Brotherhood of Humanity?" Detective Moseley asked.

"He could have joined the group to find a target to frame. And used the *Twenty Most Dangerous Survivors* posters at all the crime scenes to frame the whole group," I said.

"And all three people he killed just happened to be on the list of Survivors?" Detective Moseley asked.

"I might be able to explain that. The night of Claire's attack, I heard Richard talking to the killer. The killer was telling Richard to add someone to the list. Based on the poster found on Claire's wall he had put her name on it. He might be the one who told Richard to put all the victims on his list."

"Even if we're wrong, it's worth telling the potential victims that they might be a target," I said.

"You're right," Austin said with a smile. "It's better to be overcautious than to be called into another murder."

"Thank you." I pulled out a piece of paper from my desk. "Trevor gave me a list of the people who worked on his research. The ones who can be found easily and the ones he kept quiet."

"That's quite the list. I didn't realize so many people worked on his research," Detective Moseley said.

"It is. But if we split up the list, it shouldn't take too long." Colin and I took half the list, and Austin and Detective Moseley took the other half. I had just finished my tenth call to a young lady who helped out as a lab assistant in Trevor's research trials, when a postal worker knocked on the door.

"Ms. Bennett?" He asked.

"Yes. That's me." He handed me a long cardboard box. I signed for the box and he left.

"Who sent it?" Austin asked.

"There's no return address on the box," I said. All of us stared at the box as if it was a new toy.

"What do you think it is?" Colin asked lifting it, judging its weight in his hands and shaking it from side to side.

"No clue. Should we open it? What if it's a bomb or something?" I asked.

"Don't think so." Colin took a whiff of the box. It smells fragrant like perfume or something." I hadn't been surprised by many gifts. I try not to read people's minds in my personal life, but most people are so excited about giving gifts that they have a hard time not shouting what it is in their minds.

I tore open the paper. "Here I go," I said opening the lid. Inside the box were six long stem roses, the petals and stems had turned black and wilted. Underneath the roses was a folded-up piece of paper. After unfolding it I realized it was the same poster that was put up in my apartment from the killer, but this time the writer wrote "see you soon" across it. I saw Richard's face flash before my eyes; I dropped the note and sank deep into my chair. We didn't say anything for the longest time. The package had surprised all of us. Colin stepped out to let Gail know that a threatening package had been delivered to the office.

Then Austin put on a glove and picked up the package and note. "I think we should have the lab take a look at these. It's a long shot since they didn't find anything in your apartment, but it's worth a try."

Colin took me home and stayed with me that evening. We had the apartment to ourselves, since Molly and my mom stayed at the Survivor's Haven. We popped some popcorn and watched T.V. It felt normal. For a moment, I was able to forget everything that had happen in the last few weeks. It didn't last for long; something always seemed to pull my mind back to that night, to his face. Colin must have had the same problem, because we both stayed up until exhaustion took over and we fell asleep on the couch.

CHAPTER TWENTY-SIX

It was Austin's turn to watch over me the next evening. Colin needed a night off to be with Brittany. Based on the very loud and frequent phone calls Colin had with Brittany, I gathered that she wasn't pleased with Colin spending the night with me. Colin made reservations at Heart of Sicily, a fancy Italian restaurant and bought tickets to the play, *Beauty and the Beast* that was playing downtown.

Colin stayed with me until Austin was able to leave work. As it became closer to the time Austin was supposed to be at my apartment, Colin checked his watch every few minutes. He jumped off the sofa, when someone knocked on my door. We were both surprised to see a large bag of groceries in Austin's hands when Colin opened the door. Colin asked, "What's with the groceries, Austin?"

"I thought Claire might appreciate a home cooked meal," Austin said.

"Is there enough for three?" Colin asked.

"Wait a minute, don't you have plans this evening? Isn't that why I'm here?" Austin asked, putting the bag down on the counter in the kitchen.

"Well, yes, I guess I don't really have time to stay." Colin looked at his watch. "You kids stay out of trouble."

"You don't mind me cooking dinner, do you?" Austin asked after Colin left the apartment.

"Not at all, I was wondering what we were going to do

since I haven't had a chance to go to the store." I tried to peek in the paper bag but before I could see anything Austin moved the bag to another counter. "Do you want any help?"

"No, you can just sit at the dining room table and keep me company," he said pulling out two steaks from the paper bag.

"Did the lab have time to examine the box?" I asked.

"Yes. They didn't find anything. The only prints matched yours, the mailman, and a few other postal workers. They all had solid alibis," he said. He opened the oven and adjusted the rack. "Where do you keep your broiler?"

"In the drawer under the oven," I said.

I watched while he seasoned the steaks and put them in the oven. When he was done, he asked, "Did you find any new leads?"

"No. I'm afraid, we had no luck." I shook my head.

"We're running out of options. It's sad but we might have to wait for another crime to get more clues," Austin said.

"Well, there is one option. I know someone with the ability to read memories off objects. He might be able get the identity of the killer off objects the killer touched from the crime scenes." I decided not to tell him that it was Russ that had the ability, since he had told me in confidence.

"Why haven't you already asked him to do that?" He asked dropping corn into a pot of hot water.

"He's a teenager."

"I can see the problem. But we are running out of ways to find this guy."

"I just don't want to put him through something he isn't ready to handle. What if he sees the killer hurt someone? I know what that is like. It's not an experience I'd want to wish on a teenager or anyone else for that matter."

"Isn't it just like seeing a horror movie? It's not like the killer is hurting him," Austin said taking a seat at the dining room table.

"It varies. Reading just thoughts can be creepy but manageable. When I start picking up on feelings and memories it can get scary. It's like being trapped in someone else's body forced to experience the whole event."

"Even physically? He asked.

"Sometimes," I said.

"I never thought about how hard it is to use your side effect." Austin put a hand on my arm.

"I have learned to be more in control of my side effect. I still sometimes get trapped in a painful memory, but I can handle it. The teenager hasn't had enough time to control it. He still gets stuck in memories unable to remove himself."

"Well then don't give him an object at the crime scene. Give him the package he sent you," he said.

"Maybe."

"You should give him the choice. You might be surprised."

"I'll think about it." He nodded and went back into the kitchen to check on dinner. We talked about different styles of cooking including my mom's freestyle method while dinner finished cooking.

"This looks wonderful," I said when he brought out two plates of food.

"This is just a simple meat and potatoes meal; nothing special."

A couple of bites and I was convinced he was being modest about his cooking abilities and said so.

When he picked up my plate to take it back to the kitchen, I said, "I wish I could help. You're making me feel very guilty."

"Really? What exactly could you do with a broken wrist?"

I rubbed my cast with my good hand. "Thank you for watching me tonight."

"I'm happy to. I could understand that he needed a night off to be with his girlfriend." He started rinsing off the plates.

I laughed. "Don't let Colin hear you call Brittany his girlfriend."

"Has he ever had a girlfriend?"

"Yes. He dated the same girl all through high school."

"What happened?"

"He refused to tell us," I shrugged. "All I know is after they broke up he now has a month expiration date on all women."

"That's sad. Though I could still understand Brittany's concern, even if all they're doing is dating. You two are very," he thought for a moment and then said, "close."

"I don't understand her attitude. Of course, we are close. Colin's like family. Colin, Molly and I were in the hospital together during the plague. We were in the hospital so long; it was mostly just us and the nurses. Our parents were either sick themselves or on the other side of the quarantine. Even when Colin was just as sick as we were, he would stay up and help us through the pain. He was there when my dad died."

"I can understand how it would make you close. Amber had the plague when she was six. Aunt Pearl and my father had to go on an emergency trip to see my grandmother who was in the hospital from a heart attack. I was only thirteen, but I was the only one healthy and old enough to watch over Amber. I had to call the paramedics when Amber got sick. When I got to the hospital, the nurses told me that I couldn't see her since I hadn't had the illness yet. But, when the nurses weren't looking I ran to her room. I was exposed to the illness so they didn't let me leave the hospital until they knew I wasn't a carrier. I stayed in her hospital room for two weeks. Later I realized how foolish it was to risk getting sick myself but Aunt Pearl left me in charge of Amber and I take my responsibilities very seriously when it comes to family."

"That was very brave," I said.

"It was just the right thing to do. A child shouldn't have

to go through that alone."

After dinner we walked Rosie and sat down to play Scrabble. I was getting tired after the third game, but I was a little nervous about how we would end the evening.

"It's getting late," Austin said when he saw me yawn.

"I guess it is. I tire pretty easily these days." I rubbed my sore ribs. Austin walked me to my room. He bent down and kissed my cheek. I looped my arms around his neck and pulled him into a kiss. I felt a warm and tingly sensation run through my body. His hands started to travel down my back and I flinched slightly, when he glided over my bruised ribs. He pulled himself away and said, "I'm sorry."

"I'm not. A little pain was worth it."

"We will have plenty of time for that after you're better. When I can take you on a real date." Austin took a step back. "I'm going to stay up awhile if you need me, just wake me up."

CHAPTER TWENTY-SEVEN

I woke up early looking forward to having breakfast with Austin. When I got to the kitchen, I was shocked to see Colin making a pot of coffee. "What are you doing here?"

"I'm sorry to disappoint you," Colin said.

"Sorry, I just thought Austin would still be here."

"Austin works today. So he asked me to watch you until he gets off of work," he said pouring me a cup of coffee and handing it to me.

"How was your date?" I asked.

"I spent way too much on a small plate of food, watched a child's movie being performed by adults, just to make a woman happy, a woman who complained about the last few days up until we said goodnight when she turned into Velcro girl," he said with a long sigh.

"Ouch. I'm Sorry. Why not just break up with her?" I asked.

"Can't. Dad only lets me date the waitresses if it doesn't affect the pub. Her mood swings are hurting her performance at work. Brittany is one of the few waitresses still willing to work at the pub with the protestors outside. I agreed to keep her happy until he finds more servers," Colin said.

"Hopefully that will be soon," I said. I didn't know who I felt worse for.

"She's coming over to have dinner," he said with a

smile.

"Delightful," I said with a sigh. "I think I will stay in my room this afternoon."

I managed to stay in my room playing on my computer until the smell of hamburgers drifted in. I came out and ate dinner with Colin and Brittany. I was lucky that Brittany was still ignoring me, so I could eat in peace. After we finished dinner, Austin came to take over Colin's shift.

Austin and I took Rosie for a walk. I took him to Wonderland Bakery to pick up some cookies. Alice was delighted to meet him. When we turned to leave, she mouthed "You go, girl" to me. We spent the rest of the evening watching one of my favorite movies, the newest version of *Pride and Prejudice*. About half way through the movie he wove his fingers into mine and I laid my head on his shoulder.

He walked me to my room after the movie. He ran his fingers through my hair and kissed me softly. His hand traveled all the way down to the small of my back and I pushed myself harder into the kiss.

Austin removed himself from the kiss and cleared his throat, "Good night, Claire."

"Sweet dreams, Austin," I said with a smile before slipping into my room.

I awoke to knocking on my bedroom door. I opened it to see Austin standing there fully dressed.

"Claire, my aunt called and there was a fire at the restaurant. I need to get over there but I can't leave you alone. Shall I take you to the Haven?" Austin asked.

"No, I'd rather go with you. Just give me a minute to get dressed," I said.

I suddenly realized I was in the blue slip I wore as a nightgown on warm nights. He ran his gaze up and down before I coughed and he averted his eyes. "I will wait for you in the living room." I shut the door, and slipped on a pair of jeans and a lavender top. When I reached the living room, Austin was staring out the window. He turned around when I picked up Rosie's seatbelt harness.

"You want to take your dog?" he asked.

"I haven't left her alone since the day the killer broke into my apartment," I said.

Austin looked at Rosie's long, furry body and shook his head. When he didn't say anything, I said, "I can drive. She has already shed all over my back seat."

"No, it's fine. I need to get my car cleaned anyways," he said. From his thoughts, I could tell he was thinking of a conversation he had with Colin about my driving abilities. I let it go for now. Austin had enough to worry about.

The car ride to the restaurant was much different from the first time we drove there. I didn't need to be a mind reader to know he didn't want to talk. I didn't know what to do. I tried smiling at him the few times he took his eyes off the road, but his eyes looked right past me. Even Rosie was in her own world as she pressed her wet nose on the small opening at the top of the window in the backseat.

By the time we got there, the restaurant was gone. For a moment we took in the scene, the charred outline of the restaurant and a few appliances was all that was left of the building. The smell of ash was mixed with the salty ocean breeze. A large crowd was roaming around the parking lot. We followed the flashing lights of the ambulance parked at the back of the lot. Aunt Pearl and Amber stood behind two paramedics. When we stopped next to them, we saw that the paramedics were bandaging a man's feet.

"Aunt Pearl?" Austin asked. Aunt Pearl turned around and saw Austin. "What happened?"

"You didn't need to come all this way," Aunt Pearl said as Austin wrapped his arms around her.

"I thought I could help," he said. "I mean we."

Aunt Pearl looked at me before giving me a hug. "I'm sorry you had to come all this way. I know you're going through your own problems." She touched the top of my cast as if it was made of breakable glass.

"I'm happy to help," I said with a smile. "I'm just sorry

this happened to you."

"Tell me what happened," Austin said. He took off his navy blue jacket and wrapped it around Amber's shaking shoulders before embracing her.

"All right, but there's not much you can do now." Aunt Pearl said. "The firemen have ruled it an accident."

"It wasn't," a hoarse voice said from behind the two paramedics. The paramedics moved slightly and I realized the man sitting on the back of the ambulance was Craig the cook at the restaurant. He was a black man in his fifties covered in soot with bandages on his hands and feet. "They did it because of me. You should have just let me go."

"I'm not going to let the best cook I ever had go just to avoid a few bullies," Aunt Pearl said.

"Did you see someone start the fire?" Austin asked.

"No, but I heard voices just before I smelled the smoke. If the voices hadn't woken me up …" Craig said looking down at his bandaged hands and feet. "I just don't understand why this happened. I don't have any of the special side effects. Heck the only real talent I have is cooking, but only because I went to culinary school."

"It's not your fault." Aunt Pearl put a hand on Craig's shoulder.

"It should have been me that they went after," Amber said. "I'm …."

"Let's not talk about that right now," Austin whispered nodding his head towards the crowd of people only a few feet away.

"True. We just need to focus on rebuilding the restaurant," Aunt Pearl said.

"You're not serious?" Austin asked.

"Yes I am. We aren't just going to move," Aunt Pearl said. Aunt Pearl and Austin looked like bulls ready to charge. I decided to let the family talk amongst themselves, while I tried to listen to the thoughts of the people in the crowd. Rosie and I made our way slowly through the crowd. Most people didn't think the fire was an accident.

About half were genuinely shocked and horrified about what had happened.

When I made my way to the front of the crowd, I found four men that were radiating anger and violence. One was a fireman and the other three were wearing police uniforms. As I walked closer, I was having a hard time controlling my urge to give into the violence I was feeling by hitting them. When I calmed down, I asked the group, "What's going on here?"

"Nothing, Ma'am. Just a small fire due to wire damage," the fireman said.

"Really? Because I heard that the cook heard voices before the fire started."

"No. No one caused this fire. No need to worry." The sheriff said. I read his thoughts, *Between me and the fire chief, we'll get all the Survivors out of town.*

I went back to the ambulance. "If you don't want to move for yourself, move for Amber," Austin said.

Aunt Pearl looked at her daughter and her face softened. "Where can I go? Everywhere is risky."

"Not everywhere," I said. Everyone turned to look at me. "Gilroy is Survivor friendly. There are a few Survivor friendly neighborhoods in San Jose. My neighborhood has vacancies for both shops and apartments."

"It's something to look into," Aunt Pearl said. "It would be nice to be in an area with other Survivors for Amber."

"It's also near a nice college," Austin said.

"We should get you to the Survivor Haven for tonight. They will make room for all three of you to have a safe place to sleep," I said.

"We have a house," Aunt Pearl said.

"I don't think that's a good idea," I said looking directly at Austin.

"I agree," Austin said. "Let's get you somewhere safe. We can figure everything else out later."

"Are they going to be able to find the Haven?" I asked

when we started to drive away from the restaurant.

"Yeah, I will drive slow enough for them to follow. And we all have cell phones."

On the way to Haven, I called Gail and told her about what happened to the restaurant. I told her about what the sheriff and fire chief were doing to get the Survivors out of town. She assured me that she would handle the situation. When I hung up, I noticed Austin looking at me. He said, "Thank you."

When we got to the Haven, Molly took a look at Craig's injuries, and Abby took over in taking care of Aunt Pearl and Amber. Austin and I made it home around 4:00 am and I was grateful to be able to go back to bed.

CHAPTER TWENTY-EIGHT

The next morning, Gail poked her head in my office and said, "That little problem we discussed last night is being handled. Good work, Claire."

That was at least one worry I could let go of. I was still debating whether to ask for Russ's help or not. But I was down to my last option in trying to learn the identity of the killer. I headed to the Survivor Haven. When I got there, I found Mr. Cooper was sitting by himself reading a book.

"Mr. Cooper," I said, and he put the book on his lap.

"It's nice to see you again, Agent Bennett." He indicated for me to take a seat, so I did.

"How are you two doing?" I asked.

"Russ is doing much better. He has even found some real friends. Err not to say that his Internet friends weren't real, but uh ..." His bald head turned red.

"I know what you mean," I said looking at Russ as he sat at a table playing a card game with two other teenagers. One was a tall girl with light brown hair in braids and freckles and the other was a boy with bleached blonde hair and a cast on his right leg.

"I can't believe how many children are here," I said, scanning the rest of the room, finding a considerable number of children and teenagers. "Other than you I only see a handful of adults that aren't staff."

Mr. Cooper looked at his watch. "Most of the parents

are at work. Most of the children have one parent that stuck around, but quite a few of the children have no parents at all," Mr. Cooper said. I was feeling pretty lucky. I will have to remember to thank my mother next time I see her.

"Are you staying here much longer?" I asked.

"I hope not. We are trying to find someplace Russ would fit in better."

"I hope you find someplace soon. My neighborhood is turning into a Survivor-friendly neighborhood I'm sure there will be others. They're even putting in Survivor owned shops. There's a bakery that has the best baked goods I've ever had." I wrote down the address of the bakery and handed it to Mr. Cooper.

"I'll look into that." Mr. Cooper rubbed his belly. "If nothing else, I can't say no to a good cookie." We both laughed.

"Have you heard about the new developments in the case?" I asked, not knowing if anything had been leaked to the media.

"The detective came to tell me about what had happened to my wife and why they did it." He shook his head. "I still don't get it. I never thought they hated us that much."

"I'm afraid I have what might be bad news. We have reopened the case."

"Are you saying they didn't do it? Russ is just starting to cope with it."

"No, his aunt did play her part in the cover up of the murder but we don't think the uncle …."

He interrupted me by holding a hand up. "But she said she saw him do it and he had no alibi. He had to have done it."

"We think the killer was a Survivor that can change his appearance to look like someone else. We think the killer looked like Mike during the murder to frame him."

"Why would he do that?"

"We think he was framed because he went to a

Brotherhood of Humanity meeting and it was assumed he was a supporter of their cause."

"Well then he deserves what he got," Mr. Cooper said firmly.

"I'm not going to argue. He makes my skin crawl. That being said we still have a killer out there," I said.

"Is Russ in danger?" He asked.

I thought about that for a moment. "Russ doesn't fit the type of victim he's targeting. I couldn't say that I'm certain of that fact, but I'm pretty sure."

Mr. Cooper took a deep breath, and so did I. "I do want to ask for your permission. The killer sent me a box. It's the only evidence we have on him. We can't find any way to trace the box back to the killer. I was hoping you'd let me ask Russ if he would touch the item to see the killer's identity."

"You want him to view a killer's memories? He's only a kid."

"The box is not connected to a murder. The box would only give him the memory of the person preparing and sending the box." I hoped I was right about that. I had no reason to think the object had been at any of the crime scenes. Then again I didn't know the limits of Russ's ability.

"It's the only way?" He asked.

"The only way."

"He's going to kill again?"

"Yes." He didn't need to know it was me he was planning to kill.

"You can. But if he says no or wants to stop, you will stop."

"I promise. It's all up to Russ."

"I'll talk to him when he's done playing with his friends. If he agrees I'll send him up to your office tomorrow morning."

Abby had spotted me when I was heading for the exit. I tried to avoid eye contact. She was tiny but was faster at weaving in and out of groups of teenagers than me. She caught up with me the moment my hand touched the door to leave.

"You're fast for being injured," Abby said by my side. "I need to talk to you."

"I'm busy, can this wait?" I asked.

"It's about your mother." I hadn't expected that. I pulled my hand off the door and turned around.

"Why didn't you talk to Molly?" I asked, indicating with my head to Molly who was bandaging a boy's wrist in one of the glass offices.

"She's working," she said.

"What do you think I'm doing? Eating ice cream and watching T.V.?" She didn't have to say anything. I could read from her thoughts that she didn't want to drive Molly away because she needed her help. I, on the other hand, didn't help her so I was free to harass. "What about her?" I asked.

"She's bothering people," she said.

"That's hard to believe." I couldn't imagine she was worse than the groups of teenagers, with their eye rolling, deep sighing and girls that shrieked and screamed.

"Well believe it. She's creeping people out." The soft pink dress and perky ponytail on the top of her head may fool most, but I knew it was just to lure people in to a false sense of security. It's not to say I don't like her. Most days she's a cheerleader on Prozac, but when things don't go her way, I try not to be the person she sees first.

"I doubt my mother is creeping people out. But I'll humor you." I waved my hand to indicate she should lead. Abby led me to her office in the back of the room. She pulled the curtains to reveal a large glass window.

"Do you see her?" she asked. My mother was standing behind a large tree made of construction paper that went from the floor to the ceiling. She was writing on a small notepad. Four boys and two girls around the age of eight, sat at a table under the tree playing some board game.

"No, I have forgotten what my mother looks like." Her

eyebrows narrowed so low they almost touched. I bit my lip. I hadn't meant to say that out loud.

"Just watch." I put on a fake smile and turned to watch my mother.

I watched her write in her notepad for a few minutes. She was writing rapidly. I knew she was laughing, because her shoulder jumped and so did her mouth as she wrote.

"I'm failing to see the problem," I said after a few minutes had passed.

"Just watch." I rolled my eyes when she wasn't looking. I wonder if she knew the only creepy behavior was us watching my mom.

We watched her write for ten minutes. I was about to say a few choice words to her, when Abby said, "There, watch that." My mother wasn't doing anything, but the group of children got up from the table and moved to another table filled with paper and paint supplies. My mother closed her book and watched them leave. When the children sat down and became involved in the project, my mother slowly and carefully made her way towards them. Instead of going to their table she ducked behind a bookshelf that was placed near the table and took out her notepad and started to write.

"You don't think that's a little creepy? They're children." Abby crossed her arms and looked all too pleased with herself.

"I bet she is doing it for her job, but I'll check it out." I walked as slowly as I could to my mother. It wasn't a conversation I was looking forward to.

"Mom?" I asked as she wrote in her journal.

"Yes, dear?" Mom stood up and closed her book. "Is everything all right?"

"Everything is fine. Why are you following the children around?" That was not something I ever thought I would be asking my mother.

"I thought while I'm here I should do some work. When will I get another chance to experience firsthand how the Survivor culture started?"

"I don't think the Survivors are a culture."

"No, you're wrong. They have all had a shared traumatic experience. They are all different from the normal population. Now they are forced to interact with each other. Soon they will set rules just for themselves. I think we are seeing the first stages of a distinct culture that is forming."

She was smiling at me, her green eyes twinkling with excitement. I couldn't do it to her. "I'm happy for you, Mom. I really mean that, but try to interact with them instead of following them. If you want to listen to their conversations, ask their parents first."

"I already asked the parents. What kind of person do you think I am? Some creepy stalker?" I closed my eyes and tried to slow my racing heart. Abby must not have even talked to my mom.

"No, Mom, but she does. See that lady in the window?" I pointed at Abby, who suddenly moved away from the window. "Try to stay out of her way." Mom nodded when she grasped what I was telling her.

"How is she treating Molly?" I asked. The office Molly was in had its curtain closed. I felt guilty that we hadn't had time to talk much to each other in the past few days.

"You know Molly. She would never complain. Though I think the work is good for her and Trevor."

"I can see how it's good for her, but why Trevor?" I asked.

"It seems some of the children can see him. I've seen them talking to something just to the side of Molly. He's good with kids. Makes them laugh." I felt a twinge of pain in my heart for Trevor. The thought of him never holding his own child just broke my heart. I might have had mixed feelings about his career choices, but never about him being a father.

"Don't worry about them. For now, they're happy," my mother said as she caught me frowning.

"You're right." She hugged my good side, before walking over and sitting with the children at the table.

"My mother is not creepy." I swung Abby's office door open without knocking. "My mother is a cultural anthropologist. She's just observing how the Survivor children are coping."

"I don't care what she is. It's creepy," she said.

"My mother got parental approval. You're the only one with a problem." I started walking to the exit again.

"Now you stop right there." Abby shook her finger at me. "This is my area. If I say it's creepy then …."

"Then you deal with it. But I don't think you'll get far. Not when Gail approved us to stay here. Not when Molly, the only nurse you found willing to help, would quit." Abby didn't say anything. She folded her arms and stormed away. I was bluffing and it worked. Molly never would abandon the children. Gail would have been political and stayed out of it. I just wasn't ready to let anyone take the little joy my family had left away. We lost too much in the last few weeks. Though I wasn't sure how I felt about being good at lying, not many people could fool an empath after all. I didn't have time to worry about it; I was trying to stop a killer before he hurt anyone else in my family.

CHAPTER TWENTY-NINE

I watched the clock all morning, every tick of the minute hand reminding me it was getting closer to noon. Colin must've also been aware of the time, not because he was watching the clock but because of the sound effects I made every five minutes.

"What if he doesn't show?" I asked.

"He will show. Russ is a teenager, you can't expect him to be up before eleven if he doesn't have to be," Colin said.

The conversation was repeated every half hour. Colin was remarkably tolerant. Russ came to the office, five minutes before noon.

"Hey." He yawned, straightening his robe.

"Good morning, Russ. I knew you'd come." Russ sat in the chair across from me sliding his body down until his head rested on the back of the chair.

"You knew it?" Colin raised an eyebrow.

"I did," I said frowning slightly at Colin.

"So where's the box?" Russ asked.

I took it out of the bag that Austin brought it in. I was about to put it on the table but then drew the box back near me. "Are you sure you want to do this?"

"Yeah," he said.

"Let's try what we did last time." Russ rolled up his sleeve and put his arm on the desk. I put the box, the flowers and the note on the desk in separate spots in front of

Russ. I put my hand on his wrist. He picked up the piece of paper.

The room faded to black, and I saw a room I didn't recognize. It looked like a home office. A gloved hand was removing a piece of paper from a printer. I could hear whistling, as the person walked with the paper to a well-organized desk. A hand reached out, and it was clearly a man's hand, and grabbed a pen. Just before writing, he looked up at a picture frame. It was a picture of a girl around four years old with a small button nose and long black hair. I recognized the girl in the picture although she had looked like a boy when I saw her at the shelter. She was standing next to a woman, whose face was covered in black marker.

He looked down and wrote on the poster, "See you soon." He started whistling a new melody, I didn't recognize it but it had a country/western feel to it. Everything went black as he put the note in the box.

I kept my eyes closed. Switching from memory to memory was an odd sensation like going on a boat for the first time. I could hear the rustle of the flowers as Russ picked them up. "Gross." He sounded more intrigued than disgusted by the flowers. The image flashed again; this time it was moving fast like watching a movie on fast forward. We watched him pick the flowers, take them inside and put them in a vase on a oak dresser. I saw nothing that would be useful to our investigation. There was a break in the images. The next thing I saw was the man's hand picking up the dead flowers from the vase on the dresser. He was wearing gloves. Behind the flowers was something I couldn't quite place; it appeared to be a high-end version of a walkie talkie. When he started to walk past it, I could see it more clearly and realized it was a portable police scanner. I had seen police officers use them when we were at crime scenes.

The image stopped when he placed the flowers in the box. The image started again when Russ picked up the box. This time he was purchasing the box from a young Asian woman. We lost the images as soon as he put the box in a bag. The next images were in a completely different location. He took the box out of the bag and placed it on the table. We then saw a repeat of the piece of paper and the roses going into the box. We watched him close the box and write the address. He taped the edges down. He looked at the picture of the girl one more time before he slipped the box into a bag. The last scene with the box was him giving it to a postal worker. His gaze never strayed far enough from the box to find anything useful.

"Well that was a waste," Russ said pulling his arm away from me.

"No, not a total waste." I blinked my eyes trying to adjust to the bright lights of the office. "We might be able to use the information you found."

"We never saw the killer's face or anything else," he said.

"True, but we have more clues now than we did yesterday," I said. "By the hands we know it's a white man. And we know the man must be somehow connected to the picture he was looking at."

"I guess it's something. You'll let me know when you find him?" He asked his face softening for a brief second.

"I will." I gave him a decisive nod. "How has it been staying here at the Haven?"

"I'm going through computer withdrawal, but I've made a few friends. Here I'm not so odd – there are others just like me. Russ glanced at the clock. "Looks like I'm late for lunch so I guess I'll be going."

He dragged his feet to the door. I guess he wasn't fully awake yet.

"Thank you, Russ." He looked back at me and nodded before leaving the office.

"What did you find out? Colin asked.

"We saw a picture with a little girl and a woman whose face was crossed out. The girl was that little 'boy' you pointed out at the shelter. Maybe he has a daughter and maybe Jane Doe is his estranged wife. Though I'm not sure what that would have to do with the killings. The only real useful piece was the portable police scanner that was sitting on his dresser."

"Why would that be useful?" Colin asked. "Anyone including criminals could use a police scanner."

"True, but it's possible the killer is a police officer or firefighter or a paramedic. If he is, he might have been working at all the crime scenes," I said.

"Well, murderers have come back in the past to see the crime scenes." Colin shrugged his shoulders. "Though the few times we've seen that they have been standing with a crowd of nosy neighbors."

"It might be a long shot, but I'm out of ideas … unless you have any?" I asked.

"No, you're right. We should check out anything that comes our way," he said.

We met Austin and Detective Moseley, for an early dinner at the pub. I was pleased that the redhead waitress was serving in a different area. Instead, a man with short black hair and a hooked nose came to take our orders. Everyone ordered big plates of food. I wasn't hungry, but I ordered a hamburger and fries.

"Have you guys found anything new?" Colin asked stretching his legs onto a chair at the table beside him.

"Wish I could say we had something," Austin said. "There's just nothing to go on. We went back over all the cases, trying to find any linking physical evidence. There's just nothing, not even a print or hair that's connected."

"We may have a theory," Colin said nodding his head towards me.

"I think the killer has worked at all the crime scenes," I said.

"You think it's a cop?" Austin asked.

"I wouldn't be sharing that theory until you have proof to back it up." Detective Moseley frowned. "Cops don't take accusations like that kindly."

"I don't know if it's a cop. It could be a paramedic or

lab technician for all I know. I do think there might be a connection." I decided not to tell them how I came up with the theory. Russ had enough problems without the police knowing what he was capable of doing. His ability would be a huge asset to the police, but it just wasn't in Russ's best interest. "I'd like to see the log sheet for all three crimes. See if there is anyone that has worked at all of them."

"What would that accomplish? It's likely that more than a handful of people worked at each crime," Detective Moseley said.

"Right now just about any Survivor could be a possible suspect. I can't use my ability on everyone in town who might be a Survivor. But I could with a handful of people," I said.

"What could it hurt to try? It's not like we have any other leads," Colin said.

"They've got a point, David," Austin said.

"Hey, you want to waste your time, go for it. I'm going to stick to normal police work to solve the case," Detective Moseley said.

Austin ignored Detective Moseley and said, "I can get the case logs together and bring them to you tomorrow morning at the latest."

"Thank you." It was nice having someone believe me for a change. The news coming out about us wasn't all bad.

CHAPTER THIRTY

Colin and I went back to my apartment after dinner. Rosie was happy to see us, or at least she was happy to see the familiar white take out box from the pub, that I held in my good hand. Without asking, Rosie did every trick she knew. I gave in and gave her a small piece of hamburger, when I thought Colin wasn't looking. He did look because he soon lectured me during our walk on how bad it was to give human food to dogs.

When we got home, we got into our pajamas and settled on the couch to watch TV. Rosie nudged herself between us and laid on her back with one paw in the air. She smacked Colin with it every time he stopped rubbing her tummy. We hadn't spoken to each other since we sat down, but it was a comfortable silence. After the last show, Rosie led me to my room and I closed the door.

I was in the bathroom getting ready for bed when I heard a loud thump. I blinked and looked at the clock. It was a little after ten. I opened my bedroom door; the hallway was too dark to see anything. I heard the soft sound of chatter. Rosie sniffed the air in the hallway and started to growl. I kept my hand looped around her collar to keep her from running down the hall ahead of me.

"Colin? Is everything ok?" I asked loud enough to be heard down the hallway but not so loud that the neighbors would complain.

"Everything's fine. It's just Austin," Colin said.

"Do you need me to come out?" I asked looking down at my pajamas. They may have covered me as well as a normal pair of shorts and top, but it still felt awkward having a man I just started dating see me in them.

"No, he just brought by the crime scene logs you asked for," Colin said.

"Thanks for stopping by. I know it's late." I said.

"No problem it was on my way home," a male voice said. I felt a little guilty that he was working so late to get them to me.

When I climbed into bed, Rosie refused to leave the door to sleep in her usual spot at the foot of the bed. She paced and sniffed at the small crack under the door. I tried to sleep but Rosie started whining and digging at the deep blue carpet.

"Ok already. I'm up." She hopped around me as I put on my robe. We walked down the hallway. Colin stepped into the hallway before we reached the end. Rosie showed her teeth and started to bark and snap at Colin.

"What's with her?" Colin asked stepping back.

"She been like this since Austin knocked on the door. I don't know why she would growl at Austin. She seemed to like him before. Did he leave already?" I asked trying to look past him to the living room.

"Yeah, he got a phone call and left." My body stiffened when I looked down at Rosie, who was still trying to attack Colin, and realized what was happening. Whatever ability the killer had it didn't work on dogs.

"All right, well goodnight," I said. I forced a smile and dragged Rosie back into my room with my good arm. Just before I closed the door, I could feel something push on it from the other side. I slammed my whole body on the door and was able to push the door closed and lock it. I grabbed my phone and called Austin.

"Claire?" Austin asked.

"You need to come to my apartment. The killer is

here," I said.

"Who is it?"

"I don't know. He looks like Colin, but it's not Colin."

"I'm on my way."

"That won't keep me from coming in," Colin's voice changed to a higher octave. I recognized it instantly-it was Detective Moseley.

"Why are you doing this?" I could hear him rummaging through drawers. I was having trouble thinking between my fear and his rage.

"The news took away everything in my life. My wife left me." I saw the image of him finding an engagement ring and a wedding band on top of a letter left on a dresser. "She emptied our bank account and stole my daughter Daisy away from me." The image of him opening the door to a child's room, empty except for a child size bed and a dresser full of pulled out empty drawers, popped into my head.

I could hear the clink of a screwdriver on the door. I rushed to the bathroom with Rosie and locked the door behind us. "I'm sorry that happened to you but what does that have to do with the other people you hurt or killed?" I searched for a weapon but all I could find was hairspray and a sharp nail filer.

"You little bitch! Are you stupid? My money is gone, my baby girl is gone, my family won't even talk to me, all because of what Trevor did. The only thing I have left is my job. How much longer before they take that away too?" I could hear him open the first door.

The bathroom door was made out of cheap wood that shook as he kicked it. I backed Rosie up to the tub, so we wouldn't get hit. It only took Detective Moseley another two kicks to break the door down.

Rosie lunged at him but he kicked her to the side. "They're traitors to our kind. Because of them they hunt us down. Take our lives away. Why wouldn't they deserve to die?"

"Because they didn't hunt us down." He grabbed my

neck and pushed me to the wall. I pushed my fear to the back of my mind so I could think.

"But if they didn't say anything, we could have hidden our gifts. We could have been kings. I could have made them stay. I could have had everything." He was squeezing harder. I could hardly breathe. Rosie bit his leg. The pain caused him to momentarily loosen his grip. I managed to raise the hairspray and spray his eyes and then stab him in neck with the file. I realized I had a use for the fear I had been bottling up. I decided to try what Abby said. I let the fear flow through my fingers. He flinched away from me and fell. I ran as fast as I could, I tripped over something large in the kitchen.

I looked down and saw Colin lying motionless on the ground with a yellow file folder next to his hand. I grabbed his shoulders lightly and shook him. "Colin. Please wake up." Colin groaned.

"Claire?" His eyes opened halfway.

"We need to get out of here." I offered my good arm to Colin. He grabbed it and pulled himself off the floor. I heard Detective Moseley coming and stood up and grabbed a knife out of the drawer on the way out of the kitchen. Colin held my shoulder and stumbled beside me as we made it to the front door.

I could feel a hand grab the back of my neck as we stepped into the hallway. I swung around and stabbed the knife into his right leg and ran further down the hallway with Colin. It reminded me of the 3-legged races we ran at picnics when we were kids. I was breathing heavily which was causing pain in my ribs and chest. I couldn't calm myself down. My breathing got more and more shallow. I staggered down the hallway as my vision blurred and my legs felt unstable.

I pushed the button for the elevator, and the door opened. I lost my balance and we tumbled to the floor of the elevator. I couldn't stand up, the pain radiated throughout my body. Rosie hovered over me licking my face. I took a deep breath and rolled over to the wall as the elevator doors closed. I pulled myself up on the wall. I managed to reach the control panel and pressed both the stop and emergency buttons. That should keep us safe until help arrived. I was having trouble breathing. I fell on the ground and everything went dark.

When I opened my eyes again, I could hear chaos on the other side the door. We were still stuck between two floors and the elevator alarm was still blaring. I checked Colin but he had lapsed into unconsciousness. Rosie was whimpering beside me. I heard my name being called over the sound of the alarm.

"We're in here," I shouted.

"Are you ok?" It was Austin.

"We're alive but Colin is unconscious.

"We'll have you out in a few minutes."

"Did you capture Detective Moseley? He's the killer.

"Yes, he has already been taken away."

"OK, I'm going to lay back down now."

CHAPTER THIRTY-ONE

"I think she is coming around." I heard a squeaky voice. I felt the familiar rough texture of hospital linens on my bare legs and groaned. I recognized the doctor as Dr. Lee, the same doctor I saw the last time. "I'm glad to see you're awake, Claire. Do you know where you are?"

"Disneyland?" I coughed my chest stung but I managed to smile. Dr. Lee looked at me funny so I added, "I'm at the hospital."

"Very good. Do you remember why you're here?"

"I was attacked by a deranged detective?"

"Splendid! Your memory seems to be intact." He jotted a note in my chart. "The good news is we think you only broke a rib, but now that you're awake we'd like to run some tests on you."

As I became more alert, I started to realize something was missing in my memory. "Where's Colin? Where's my dog?" I asked trying to sit up but finding my body was too weak.

"I don't know about your dog, but Colin only suffered a minor concussion. I'm going to let some people in who have been waiting to see you is that ok? Are you up for it?" he asked.

"Yes." My voice was hoarse and shaky.

"You know when you begin to be on a first name basis with the E.R. doctors, because of on the job injuries, most people see it as a sign to change careers," he said with a soft smile. I laughed and it hurt from the inside out, but it felt good somehow.

My mother came in the room first and sat next to me, brushing the hair out of my face. Colin and Austin followed her, both edging the other out to get in the door first. Colin won by a nose.

"How are you doing?" Colin asked.

"I have had better days." I said. "How are you?"

"Ok, so that was a silly question. Gail stopped by but couldn't stay. She says we're on the disabled list until we are cleared by the doctor and have been checked out by the department shrink. From the looks of things I'll be back at work long before you are," Colin said.

"We were so worried," Austin said holding my hand.

"What will happen to the men in prison?" I asked.

"It's going to take some time to work out the legal process of showing this type of evidence, but we think we can get them out in a few weeks with your testimony and the officer's testimony of what happened today," Austin said.

"How are you going to keep Detective Moseley in jail when he can look like any of the guards?" I asked.

"He can only make one person at a time see him as someone else. We discovered that when we arrived on the scene and one of the officers saw Detective Moseley and the other saw an elderly man, both with knife wounds in their leg. So as long as there are two guards with him at all times, we should be ok."

I thought for a moment. He was right; there was never more than one other person near the killer during each crime.

At that point, my mom decided there were too many people in the room and shooed everyone else out.

The next morning I managed to escape my room while my mother was getting coffee and walk down the hall to the room of Susanna Russo, now known as Emily Moseley. Pastor Doyle was still there. He looked much happier and reported that Emily was doing much better. With the arrest of her husband, Laura brought Daisy out of hiding and they were both staying with Pastor Doyle.

My mother took me home the next day and stayed with me, since I wasn't up to taking care of myself with only one functioning leg and arm. My mother hovered around me every chance she could. She even slept next to me as if I might die if she left me. Rosie hadn't been hurt so she also hovered, so close that she crushed me from time to time. Molly spent most of her time helping out at the Haven but came home whenever she got time off.

After a few days I started missing Colin and Austin. Then I discovered that they had tried to stop by but my mom wouldn't let them in. I made sure I was awake the next time they came by and was rewarded with two bouquets of flowers. They still didn't stay long with my mother glaring at them the whole time. I read the cards that came with the flowers after they left. Austin's said, "I'm looking forward to having a real second date with you when you are better". Colin's card said, "Get well soon. The paperwork is really stacking up."

By the end of the first week, I was getting bored and cranky. Mom suggested that we work on turning the third bedroom into a nursery as a surprise for Molly. What a fun project! It really brightened my days to think about the future and not the past. With my injuries still healing, Mom had to do most of the hard work but I sure enjoyed looking through the catalogues and picking out baby accessories. It was too early to know the gender so we went with multicolored pastels to be safe.

We asked Molly to come home for dinner on Thursday to celebrate my recovery. It was the only way we could be sure that she'd be at home at a particular time so we could surprise her with the nursery. Predictably, she burst into tears as soon as she saw it. Looking to the future is both happy and sad for her with Trevor not able to fully participate.

"Trevor says the room is beautiful and I should stop crying."

"For once, Trevor and I are in agreement. You need to look forward for both your sake and the baby's," I said.

"I wonder if the baby will take after you or Trevor," Mom said.

"I'm hoping for Molly's looks, no offense, Trevor," I said. Molly blushed. I'm guessing Trevor is also hoping the baby is as beautiful as Molly.

Then I remembered the discussion we had with Trevor about genetics. "Molly, what side effect did Trevor have?"

"I don't remember him ever telling me. Trevor?" Molly asked. She repeated what Trevor said to us, "He says he won't tell us. Why did you want to know?"

"Remember, Trevor told us that it's possible that our side effects can be inherited," I said.

"Wow!" She took a seat in the new rocking chair. "That is something I hadn't even considered. Parenting is hard enough without special abilities."

"Think of it as an adventure – that's what I did," Mom said.

"I guess we'll just have to wait and see how my niece or nephew turns out," I said, putting a hand on Molly's shoulder.

I was cleared to go back to work on Monday. On Sunday, Colin came by to take me for a walk around the neighborhood. I wasn't sure whether it was for my company or to make sure I was really ready to go back to work.

"I know you haven't gone very far from the apartment yet so I have something to show you," Colin said.

"Are you sure you have the time, I thought this was red-headed waitress's night off."

"Oh, we broke up last week."

"Why?" I smiled and then immediately pulled my lips into a frown. "Should I be sad?"

"No, she was a little more clingy than I could tolerate. Besides, Dad finally hired a new waitress."

We reached the end of the block and turned the corner. I saw that the next three blocks were cordoned off by construction fences.

"What's going on here?" I asked.

"A lot of people and businesses moved or closed up because they didn't want to be so close to so many Survivors. Mr. Cooper and other Survivors and Survivor supporters are buying up the land to extend this Survivor-friendly neighborhood. The goal is to have a self-sufficient Survivor friendly town someday," Colin said. We stood there for a while, amazed at how much our neighborhood had changed in a matter of weeks.

The next morning I got a call before I left the apartment. Instead of going to the office, I was to meet Colin and Austin at a large pond in the middle of Coyote Park just outside of town. The pond didn't look right as I walked up to it. Then I realized it was frozen. A long hand could be seen reaching out on top of the ice with the rest of the body in the ice.

Colin and Austin were already there along with the crime lab folks. As I walked up, Colin was saying to Austin, "Yes, that's why we were assigned this case. A frozen lake with a body in it in the middle of August clearly involves at least one Survivor."

"OK, boys, let's get to work," I said with a smile.

THE PUZZLE KEEPER